ABOUT THE MURDER OF
GERALDINE FOSTER

ABOUT THE MURDER OF GERALDINE FOSTER

ANTHONY ABBOT

COACHWHIP PUBLICATIONS
GREENVILLE, OHIO

TO THE
STANDING ARMY
OF THE
CITY OF NEW YORK—
THE POLICE DEPARTMENT

About the Murder of Geraldine Foster, by Anthony Abbot
© 2026 Coachwhip Publications edition

First published 1930
Fulton Oursler, 1893-1952
CoachwhipBooks.com

ISBN 1-61646-637-5
ISBN-13 978-1-61646-637-4

PIGEONS FROM HELL: ANTHONY ABBOT'S
ABOUT THE MURDER OF GERALDINE FOSTER

Curtis Evans

1930 was an epochal year in the history of American crime fiction, for it saw the continued rise to preeminence of hard-boiled crime writer Dashiell Hammett and the beginning of the decline of classic detective fiction guru S. S. Van Dine. In 1928 and 1929 Van Dine, a.k.a. popular critic and general know-all Willard Huntington Wright, had hit the American bestseller lists with his much-lauded detective novels *The Greene Murder Case* and *The Bishop Murder Case*, the third and fourth installments in his Philo Vance mystery series, both of which charted at the position of number four. It was an almost unheard-of achievement up to that time, strange as it may seem today, for a mystery novel to achieve bestseller status in the United States. Way back in 1902 Arthur Conan Doyle had managed it with his classic Sherlock Holmes detective novel *The Hound of the Baskervilles* (it reached the number seven spot), as had Mary Roberts Rinehart in 1910 with the railroad mystery *The Man in Lower Ten* (number four) and E. Phillips Oppenheim a full decade later in 1920 with the espionage thriller *The Great Impersonation* (number eight); but these were rare feats indeed at the time. Counting Van Dine's twofer placement, such a thing happened in merely five respective years over the first three decades of the twentieth century. Van Dine was the first and only mystery writer to

5

achieve two bestselling mystery novels until 1930, when grande dame Mary Roberts Rinehart scored again, after a lapse of two decades, with her mystery *The Door* (number six). Immediately consecutive appearances by a mystery writer other than Van Dine would not be achieved until a decade had elapsed, when Daphne Du Marier in 1938 and 1939 respectively hit numbers four and three with the same novel, her classic Gothic chiller *Rebecca*.

In 1929, no fewer than three talkie films were made from the second, third, and fourth Philo Vance detective novels while in 1930 another flick was made from the first one. Three of these films starred William Powell as Vance (in the other one a pinch-hitting Basil Rathbone took on the role), making the debonair, mustached actor a major American movie star. Yet in 1930 Van Dine's fifth Philo Vance detective novel, *The Scarab Murder Case*, though like its predecessors successfully serialized in a slick magazine and quite popular, would fail similarly to achieve bestseller status; and it would go unfilmed (and then indifferently) until 1936. To be sure, Van Dine after a three-year hiatus would publish in 1933 another well-received Vance mystery, *The Kennel Murder Case*, and a successful film, again starring William Powell and widely regarded as the best installment in the movie series, would be adapted from *Kennel* the same year, but Van Dine in truth had achieved his plateau as a mystery writer, both critically and popularly, back in 1929.

That same year, not altogether coincidentally, saw Dashiell Hammett, a tough private eye mystery scribbler from the pulps, achieve strong critical notice with his novels *Red Harvest* and *The Dain Curse* (particularly the former). In 1930 Hammett published the landmark hard-boiled Sam Spade PI crime novel *The Maltese Falcon*, and the mystery genre was never the same again. Hard-fisted crime novels set in mean streets became legion in America, while the supremacy of the cozier classic country house mystery waned. Hammett himself would burn out after in 1934 publishing the quippy "couple" detective novel *The Thin Man*, which spawned the hugely popular Thin Man film series, starring as Nick and Nora Charles none other than William Powell (who bailed out on the Van Dine mystery films) and Myrna Loy. Yet hard-boiled writers like Hammett—Hammett's shadows, one might say—were very much here to stay.

All of this notwithstanding, however, Van Dine certainly had his followers in America, the most significant of whom was Ellery Queen (pen name of the brothers Fredric Dannay and Manfred Lee), who published *The Roman Hat Mystery* in 1929, at the height of Van Dine's prestige. Ellery Queen essentially replicated the Van Dine formula, though "he" in fact was a far more ingenious and crafty crime writer than his illustrious predecessor. Van Dine introduced a suave dilettante New York City amateur detective, Philo Vance, who invariably had to "show the way" to stumbling New York City District Attorney John F. X. Markham. Vance's brilliant investigative and deductive feats were chronicled by his doggedly loyal friend, S. S. Van Dine himself, or Van as he is called in the books. Rather similarly Ellery Queen is a dilettante mystery writing amateur detective, the son of Inspector Richard Queen of the New York Homicide Squad. The Ellery Queen mystery series went on to outlast Van Dine, who died in 1939, by over three decades and spawned a much-admired though short-lived television series in the 1970s.

Van Dine's most significant follower after Ellery Queen was Anthony Abbot, pen name of journalist Fulton Oursler. Oursler, who wrote the hit stage mystery melodrama *The Spider* in 1927, as Anthony Abbot—a name he chose, he later said, because it was guaranteed to appear first on bookstore and library shelves—published, beginning

with *About the Murder of Geraldine Foster* in 1930, eight
Thatcher Colt detective novels and two novellas, all of
which, with the exception of the two last novels, which
were published respectively in 1939 and 1943, followed
the "About the . . ." pattern with their titles. Oursler was
also one of the writers who participated in the composi-
tion of the novelty round robin mystery novel *The President's Mystery Story* (1935), a.k.a. *The President's Mystery
Plot*, which was inspired by a plot proposed to him by then
American president Franklin D. Roosevelt.

About the Murder of Geraldine Foster, which was
much-lauded in its day by crime fiction critics, got the
Thatcher Colt series off to a strong start. Like Ellery
Queen, Anthony Abbot to a considerable extent imitat-
ed the tried-and-true Van Dine detective fiction formula,
particularly with the earlier novels in the series. In *Geraldine Foster* Thatcher Colt is introduced to readers as a
privileged New York City sophisticate like Philo Vance
and Ellery Queen, though he is no amateur like those men
but rather none other than Police Commissioner of the
City of New York. His sleuthing exploits are narrated by
his loyal secretary, Anthony Abbott, known as Tony, who
is nearly as worshipful of his idol as Van is of his. Colt, we
learn, is handsome and virile, a heroic Great War veteran,
yet, like the "aesthetic" Vance, not a hint of interest does
the seemingly confirmed bachelor evince in the opposite
sex during the course of the Gerladine Foster case. (Tony,
on the other hand, quickly becomes smitten with a comely
female suspect.)

Tony lets us know that Colt like Vance is a brilliant
criminologist, possessing a library of "more than fifteen
thousand books on crime and its related topics." The
Police Commissioner casually uses tongue-twisting words
which no one knows the meaning of (like "xerophilous")
though in contrast with Vance he does not affectedly drop

his "g's." "[N]ot since the days of Theodore Roosevelt," we
are breathlessly informed, has the city "known a chief of
such strength, courage and decision." Further, the chief is
"the best dressed man in public life" and in his off hours
composes sonnets and villanelles and plays cadenzas on his
flute. At home he dons a "dressing gown of strong, rich
silk, a flowered paduasoy." Honestly, if this gent had a
posh-off with Philo Vance I am not sure which toff would
win the green carnation.

The case in which Thatcher Colt involves himself, much
to the irritation of his nemesis, posturing political District
Attorney Merle Doughtery (here again Abbot follows Van
Dine, though Van Dine's John F. X. Markham is a more
sympathetic character, Doughtery being more or less a

complete buffoon), concerns the disappearance, on Christmas Eve, of Geraldine Foster, the attractive receptionist at a
handsome society doctor's office. At the time of her vanish-
ing, Geraldine shared an apartment with her pretty friend
Betty Canfield and was engaged soon to be married to a
nice young bond salesman. Betty is a good girl, her father
emphatically assures Colt. So, when Geraldine is discovered, along with a small flock of seven dead, blood-
engorged pigeons, brutally hacked to death at a lonely

house, the question becomes who on earth would want so savagely to murder this seemingly inoffensive receptionist? It proves a complex question indeed, one finally impressively elucidated by Thatcher Colt after DA Doughtery has made a downright mess of things.

Choctaw mystery writer and critic Todd Downing, a great fan of complex, outré mystery writers like Van Dine, Ellery Queen, and John Dickson Carr, was one of the notable admirers of Anthony Abbot. Reviewing *Geraldine Foster* in the Oklahoma City *Daily Oklahoman*, Downing enthusiastically observed: "What makes this story linger in the memory of the reader is the element of horror which permeates the tale, from the finding of several dead pigeons to the final revelation of the manner in which Gerladine met her death. . . . Colt uncovers one of the most fiendish crimes ever committed in fact or fiction." And, indeed, the novel is informed by true crime cases, of which Anthony Abbot, like his creation Thatcher Colt, seems to have had an encyclopedic knowledge. Abbot's interest in true crime would again be evident in the fine second novel in the series, *About the Murder of the Clergyman's Mistress*, which was inspired by one of the most notorious crimes of the Roaring Twenties, a decade which certainly experienced more than its share of sensational murders.

Another interesting aspect of the *Geraldine Foster* is its exposure of dubious American police interrogation methods from that bygone era, including the infamous third degree and employment of lie detectors and scopolamine, or truth serum. Although Abbot does not condemn any of these practices through the voice of Thatcher Colt, he does have his sleuth condemn the basic unfairness to accused criminals of the grand jury system, under which a prosecutor notoriously could secure an indictment against a ham sandwich. "Almost always, Dougherty, or any other

District Attorney, can get the indictment he wants," complains Colt, no matter how deficient the evidence presented against the person concerned. "The whole system is wrong. . . ."

Fulton Oursler, the man behind Anthony Abbot, would go on to become senior editor of *Reader's Digest* in 1944, after which he ceased writing Thatcher Colt mysteries. As Anthony Abbot he published in 1947 an article in *Reader's Digest* about a 1924 murder case that inspired the Elia Kazan film *Boomerang* (1947), about a Connecticut prosecutor who entered a declaration of *nolle prosequi,* voluntarily ending the state's case against a defendant whom he believed was innocent. Oursler converted to Catholicism in 1943 and he would author the hugely popular religious novel *The Greatest Story Ever Told* in 1949. Three years later Oursler died at the age of fifty-nine, leaving behind, in addition to religious writing of more recent vintage, a significant crime fiction legacy which richly merits rediscovery.

NOVELS

About the Murder of Geraldine Foster (1930)
About the Murder of the Clergyman's Mistress (1931)
About the Murder of the Night Club Lady (1931)
About the Murder of the Circus Queen (1932)
About the Murder of a Startled Lady (1935)
About the Murder of a Man Afraid of Women (1937)
The Creeps (1939)
The Shudders (1943)

NOVELETTES

"About the Disappearance of Agatha King" (1939)
"About the Perfect Crime of Mr. Digberry" (1940)

ABOUT THE MURDER OF GERALDINE FOSTER

PREFACE

When Mr. Thatcher Colt was Police Commissioner of the City of New York he was confronted with a number of mysterious crimes. In the face of grave difficulties, not all of which were known to the public, he personally conducted the investigations and, under handicaps that might have discouraged a less determined man, he solved the cases, arrested the guilty persons and saw them convicted. Yet the credit for his detective work was given to others. Recently we approached Mr. Colt with the proposal that the facts in these startling cases be published. At first he declined, on the wholly reasonable grounds that it might appear he was seeking honor for himself. The argument which finally persuaded the former commissioner was that he would bring honor to a place where it is too often a stranger—the police department.

It is all too true that the American public does not sufficiently appreciate its police. There is a romantic fallacy that the Force is hopeless when faced with a clever crime; indeed many persons hold the departments of the country in contempt and derision. From short stories and novels they seem to have gained the impression that puzzling crimes are solved only by brilliant amateurs. These whimsical creatures of the story-teller's imagination, a printed army of amiable dilettantes of the current fiction, are gentlemen of inexhaustible knowledge and accomplishment. They are experts in chemistry and astronomy, psycho-analysis and fire-arms; they know rugs, music, chess and wines; they are languid fellows with a great fund of humor, and a mischievous liking for cryptic utterances until they are ready to put a delicate finger on the malefactor. Their avocation is to catch elusive murderers, when the police detectives are ready to confess their utter ineptitude for their own business.

Of course there are no such detectives in real life. Yet the crimes of reality are infinitely stranger than the fanciful misdeeds which these imaginary detectives are asked to unravel. The police face crime and mystery as a part of their daily routine, and they solve their cases by knowing their business and attending to it—by vast and competent organization, patience and determined hard work, together with some ingenuity and an occasional streak of good luck. We should not be deluded into believing that such men are incompetent or corrupt.

True, a police department is seldom stronger than its chief. But it is also true that New York has been fortunate in its succession of Commissioners, from Woods and Roosevelt down to the latest reign of Whalen and Mulrooney. They, and those officers who came in between—Enright, who started as a patrolman, pounding the curb, McLoughlin who was himself a fine detective, and Warren (whose real story, also, has never been told) and the others, were honest and able officials.

Greater than any of these was Thatcher Colt, greater because of his peculiar fitness for the job. A man born to wealth, family and position, he made crime his hobby while he was still in college. He knows the modern criminology in all its schools, from Lombroso to Adler. He is never afraid, as you will see, to try new methods, and preserves an open mind until all the evidence is in his hands.

More, Thatcher Colt is an historian of crimes, often an invaluable asset to a detective. It is amazing how many crimes are duplicated, especially murders—killers seem to plagiarize from the past. The details of a thousand bloody old deeds are at Thatcher Colt's finger-tips.

We asked the former Commissioner to tell his own story, but unfortunately his present work, as a private investigator, made that impossible. However, his young secretary, Mr. Anthony Abbot, has undertaken the task with a high enthusiasm that springs from his admiration for his chief. For his first account, Mr. Abbot selected the bewildering and brutal murder of Geraldine Foster. The public was left in doubt about the case; the essential facts were withheld, and for an excellent reason. It is still regarded as one of the classic cases of the department—a crime of unexampled ferocity and cunning, surrounded by mysterious circumstances and planned and executed as if with the cold savagery of an inspired lunatic. Here was a ready-made opportunity for the gifted amateur sleuths of the metropolis, but the mystery was finally solved by the logical agency for such gruesome business, the police department, under the direction of its Commissioner, Mr. Thatcher Colt.

The Publishers.

I
MISSING!

The disappearance of Geraldine Foster was first reported to the authorities on the third day after Christmas, several years ago.

Only a desk-lamp was burning in that famous private office at the north end of the second floor of Police Head-quarters at 240 Centre Street, New York City. The rest of the Commissioner's room was darkened with the premature shadows of a raw and gusty winter afternoon. Brooding over a shuffle of blue-prints, Thatcher Colt sat at his desk, enchanted with the traffic puzzle of a great city.

Finally he glanced up at me quizzically.

"You can go, Tony," he said. "You've done enough work for one secretary today."

"Captain Henry wants to see you, but I told him you didn't wish to be disturbed," I replied.

"Oh, well—send him right in."

Captain—now Deputy Inspector—Israel Henry was in charge of the cluster of offices surrounding the private room of the Police Commissioner of New York City. In this capacity he was the guardian of Thatcher Colt's privacy and all visitors had to see him first.

Responding to my call, Henry marched into the office, a heavy-set, silver-haired police captain, and, saluting, laid an opened envelope before Thatcher Colt.

"Young lady brought this in. Been waiting an hour. Says she won't go away until you've looked at it yourself."

Thatcher Colt read the letter with deep attention. Under the lamp-light, the Commissioner was a striking figure, with his huge and powerful frame and soldier's face. He was the best dressed man in public life, and regarded by the more frivolous newspapers as a *flaneur* or, at best, a dilettante in crime, yet not since the days of Theodore Roosevelt had the Department known a chief of such strength, courage and decision. His black hair was crisp and closely cut, his brown eyes somber and resolved and in his firm features lived action and authority.

Having read the letter, Thatcher Colt picked up the telephone.

"Is Captain Laird still in the building? . . . Helloa, Captain . . . Young lady in my office—sent to me by one of my oldest friends. Mind if we talk with her together? Come right up."

Meanwhile, Captain Henry had led in the girl whom he introduced as Miss Betty Canfield. She had an attractive and piquant face and exceedingly large brown eyes, and she was becomingly dressed in a squirrel coat, saucy blue hat and the smallest snake-skin shoes I had ever seen. As I brought forward a chair, Thatcher Colt greeted her pleasantly.

"So you are the niece of Frank Canfield," he began. "It will be a pleasure to do anything I can for you. Do I understand one of your friends is missing?"

"My roommate," said Betty Canfield, with a catch in her voice.

The door opened then to admit Captain Laird, a tall, slender, keen-eyed officer in middle years. Laird was one of the first university men to choose a career in the Police Department. At Dartmouth he had been a track star and now the thirty-four detective sergeants under his command were all athletes. Addressing Betty Canfield, Thatcher Colt explained:

"Captain Laird is the chief of our Missing Persons Bureau. More than three thousand disappearance cases are reported to his office every year and he manages to account for an average of 98 per cent of them—so you've come to the right place."

Betty Canfield's expressive glance toward Captain Laird was full of appeal.

"However, our most difficult cases," admonished Thatcher Colt, "are those in which the family or friends give only a part of the truth, and not all. So tell us everything."

With admirable directness, Betty Canfield related a curious story. For three years she had been sharing a small apartment on Morningside Heights with Geraldine Foster, a girl of about her own age, who worked in a doctor's office in Washington Square. Recently the two girls had agreed to separate, because Geraldine was planning to be married, the date having been set for January 2. The last time the two had been together was around noon on the previous Saturday, which was Christmas Eve, when they lunched at the Hotel Brevoort and then looked at a one-room apartment in East Tenth Street which Betty had decided to lease.

"I said good-bye to Geraldine at the southeast corner of Fifth Avenue and Tenth Street. Suddenly she leaned forward and kissed me and she said, 'If I don't come home for supper, Betty, don't be worried—I'll be doing my Christmas shopping.' And before I could answer she had crossed the Avenue and was walking down toward Washington Square."

"And you haven't heard from her since?" asked Thatcher Colt, filling his pipe.

"I talked with her later that afternoon over the telephone and, Mr. Colt, it was that last conversation which makes me feel so frightened."

"Why, how is that?"

"I called Geraldine to tell her about a Christmas bonus that our firm had given to the employes. I waited for an hour, because Geraldine had said the doctor would be out at that time. I could tell by her voice that she had been crying and I asked her what was the matter. She admitted that she and Doctor Maskell had quarreled. But she wouldn't tell me why."

"Doctor Maskell!" reflected Colt aloud. "Is he related to George Maskell, the criminal lawyer?"

"I understand they are brothers," said Betty.

"A very distinguished family," interposed Captain Laird. "And a queer one. George Maskell is the Robin Hood of the radicals—he and his wife, who is his law partner, represent rich clients at enormous fees and then work for radicals for nothing. They were also associated with Clarence Darrow and Arthur Garfield Hays, in the Grecco-Carillo murder case."

"I remember," nodded Colt. "Doctor Maskell must be a rich man."

"Geraldine told me he will be rich when his father dies," explained Betty Canfield. "The two sons will inherit millions then. But neither of them has much now, I understand."

"About what time was it when you had this telephone conversation with your roommate."

"It was exactly three o'clock."

"What makes you so precise on that point?"

"I waited until that exact time to telephone, so that I could avoid talking to Doctor Maskell—I have never liked the man."

"Still, you haven't told me how you knew when it got to be three."

"Oh! There is a little clock on my desk—Geraldine gave it to me last Christmas—I was looking at the dial all the time I was waiting for the number to answer."

"I see. Now tell me what was said further between yourself and Geraldine, over the telephone."

"After Geraldine said she had been quarrelling, I didn't have the heart to talk about the bonus, but I told her if she would come home to supper, I would go out shopping with her. But all she answered was, 'Christmas doesn't hold anything for me now, Betty. I wish to God I was dead. And I guess I soon will be. Betty, you may never see me again as long as you live.' And then she burst out laughing and said she knew she was acting like a fool and promised to be home early."

"But she did not come home?"

Betty Canfield shook her head and swallowed hard.

"No! But I wasn't much worried because she often stayed away from the apartment for weekends and holidays, without telling me in advance. I supposed she had gone over to her folks in New Jersey."

"What time did you leave your office on Christmas Eve?" asked Colt.

"About four o'clock."

"And where did you go then?"

"From one shop to another—why?"

"It is possible then that Geraldine might have tried to telephone you later and failed to connect—isn't it?"

"Yes. I figured just that way. But when Monday came and I hadn't heard from her, I telephoned her mother in Millbrink, New Jersey. Mrs. Foster told me she had expected her for Christmas dinner, and was surprised when she did not even telephone. A week before they had arranged the plan for her to spend the holiday with the family. But they weren't really worried, either. She was an impulsive creature, and had often disappointed them. They supposed she went to Boston to spend Christmas with the family of her fiancé, Harry Armstrong. Well, I telephoned Harry, only to find out that he hadn't heard from her either, not since Friday night when he said good-bye to her in Grand Central Station and took the train for Boston. Then I called up Doctor Maskell. He says that when he returned to his office on Christmas Eve afternoon, he found the rooms locked up. Geraldine had left without any note or message of explanation to him and without waiting for her salary."

"What did her parents say about that?" asked Thatcher Colt, with an intent glance.

"They kept expecting to hear from her in every mail. But old Mr. Foster began to feel upset when I called again yesterday, and this afternoon, when there was still no word, he became really alarmed. He is on his way to New York now and will be at my apartment tonight. I told him I was coming down here and he asked me to tell you that he would offer a thousand dollars reward, if you thought that would help."

Thatcher Colt lit his pipe and sat back in his chair.

"We have many cases where nice and sensible girls act queerly just before their marriage," he mused. "How old is Geraldine?"

"Twenty-two."

"Have you a picture of her?"

Opening her purse, Betty laid before the Police Commissioner a cabinet photograph in a decorative folder. Captain Laird and my chief studied it intently, and from my chair beside the desk I also could see it easily—the face of a good-humored, intelligent and quite lovely girl.

Still studying the portrait attentively, Thatcher Colt asked for a detailed description, always a difficult thing to obtain. Coloring, height and weight are details about which one's friends usually are vague; people come to Headquarters to start a search with only dim images in their minds of their nearest relatives. Finally, Betty Canfield fixed on the following description:

Geraldine Foster was five feet, five inches tall, and weighed 130 pounds. She had light brown hair, running to reddish, and blue-grey eyes. One of her notable characteristics were long, slender and beautifully kept hands. On the fourth finger of the left hand she wore a diamond engagement ring. When last seen by Miss Canfield, she was wearing a brown beaver coat, a close-fitting orange and brown toque, flesh-colored stockings, brown shoes, brown gloves and bag.

Having jotted down these data, Thatcher Colt asked:

"Were any of Miss Foster's clothes, suit-cases or other effects missing from your apartment?"

"No, sir. Wherever Geraldine went, she took nothing with her. As a matter of fact—"

Betty stood up and came nearer to Thatcher Colt.

"It may not have any significance," she said, "but it struck me awfully queer. The night before Christmas Eve—Friday night—Geraldine had gone to the theatre with Harry Armstrong, the young man she is going to marry. After the show, she came home very low in spirits, and sat down on her trunk and suddenly she said to me that she was sick of the sight of her honeymoon clothes."

"That was odd! Do you think she was the sort of a girl who might get despondent and—"

"Never, Mr. Colt. Geraldine had a peculiar horror of death. She would cross the street rather than walk by an undertaker's. I think her mother had something to do with that. The old lady considers herself a spirit medium. She spends hours in the dark making the parlor table bounce around."

Captain Laird looked at his watch.

"It is now 5:30," he said. "I shall get started on this at once."

"Please tell me what you are going to do," asked Betty earnestly.

"We will check up on all the current reports in the Bureau of Information downstairs. In that way, we can see if any unidentified girls have met with accidents since Christmas Eve. Also whether any girl was arrested and gave a fake name and address. Then we will also check up on the hospitals for reports of amnesia and aphasia cases."

But Captain Laird refrained from telling Betty Canfield that his men would also be peering down through the icy shelves of the Morgue.

"Thanks, Captain Laird," said the girl gratefully, as the tall officer bowed and left the room.

Thatcher Colt was re-loading his pipe.

"What time do you expect Geraldine's parents at your apartment?" he asked.

"Around nine o'clock. I can bring them here if—"

"No. Instead, I would like to pay a visit to your apartment tonight, if you don't mind. You see, I take a more personal interest in this case because of my long friendship with your uncle. If you don't object, I'd like to look over your premises a bit. Mind?"

"Not at all," answered Betty. "I am happy that—"

"Now, this doctor that Geraldine worked for. What was his full name and address?"

"Doctor Humphrey Maskell. His office is at 186 Washington Square, North, but he lives at a hotel on lower Fifth Avenue."

"What did Geraldine do in Doctor Maskell's office? Was she a nurse?"

"No. She was a reception clerk for his patients, kept his account books, mailed out his bills—"

"I see. One more question. Mind?"

"I'll tell you everything I can."

"Who was Geraldine's dentist?"

Betty Canfield's face was full of bewilderment as she replied that Geraldine's teeth were cared for by a certain

Doctor Morton, in West End Avenue. I could see that she had no inkling as to the purpose of Thatcher Colt's question. Dead bodies, so decomposed as to be unrecognizable, are often identified by dental signs and tokens.

"Why didn't you like Geraldine's employer?" asked Thatcher Colt, suddenly.

Betty's dark eyes flashed.

"The reason why I cannot tell," she quoted from the old rune about Doctor Fell. "I mean I dislike him instinctively—without any real reason whatever. But there must be something wrong with a man whose own father and brother won't have anything to do with him."

"Thanks, Miss Canfield. Stop worrying and we'll try to find your friend. Give my best to your uncle—and expect us about eight tonight. The address?"

She gave the number of the Esplanade, an apartment house on Morningside Drive, and had reached the door when Thatcher Colt called out:

"Miss Canfield, would you mind telling me what you and Geraldine had for lunch on Christmas Eve at the Brevoort?"

The girl's eyes held a startled gleam as she considered for a moment. Had she possibly divined the gruesome import of the Commissioner's question? Then she answered:

"We had snails, Mr. Colt. Why do you ask?"

"Thanks, and *au revoir,*" and Thatcher Colt picked up his desk telephone.

Betty Canfield gave me an inquiring glance, for which I was deeply grateful; it was the first time she had looked in my direction. Then she turned and the door of Thatcher Colt's office closed behind her. The Commissioner was talking into the inter-office telephone.

"Have Inspector Ruggles come in."

While he was waiting, Thatcher Colt reread the note
that Betty Canfield had brought him. His somber brown
eyes were exceedingly thoughtful, as if he were turning
over in his mind some indeterminate project. When Ruggles entered the Commissioner gave him crisp orders:

"Send a detective over to the office of Doctor Humphrey Maskell at 186 Washington Square, North. Find
out what he knows about the disappearance of a girl who
worked in his office. Her name was Geraldine Foster."

"Okay," replied Ruggles heavily. He turned and strode
toward the door when the Commissioner unexpectedly
barked at him:

"Never mind, Ruggles. Forget it!"

The inspector is a model of discipline for the whole
Department. Showing no surprise whatever, he quietly
acquiesced and departed without another word.

The Commissioner was again talking on the telephone.

"Doctor Humphrey Maskell? This is the Police Commissioner speaking. Could you arrange to be in your office
if I dropped in around ten o'clock tonight? Mind? Thank
you."

Turning from the telephone, Thatcher Colt said to me:

"Pretty little thing, that Betty Canfield, eh, Tony?"

"Check and double check," I agreed with emphasis.

"Looks like a little beaver with those bright eyes."

It is a habit of Thatcher Colt to compare human beings
to animals, birds or fishes—every face he sees suggests to
him a parallel from natural history.

"But she didn't tell us all she knows, Tony," added the
Commissioner with a sigh. "Nice, sweet girl, from a good
family, but she comes down here and tells me lies. That's
too bad."

"But, chief, how did she—"

Thatcher Colt waved my question aside. Bending again
over his traffic blue-prints, he added:

"Get your dinner, Tony, and meet me at the garage in an hour. I noticed how you admired my friend's niece, so I am taking you up there with me tonight."

2
THE GIRL WHO ASKED FOR MONEY

What had made Thatcher Colt believe that Betty Canfield had lied to him?

Over my solitary dinner in a Pearl Street lunchroom, I puzzled that question with knitted brows but came no nearer to the answer. It was generally that way when I tried to follow the strange thoughtways of the Police Commissioner. In all the years that I had known him, he had invariably baffled me, and yet I was closer to him than any other person. During those days at Headquarters, and especially during the Geraldine Foster excitement, his political enemies all said his personal activities in the case were mostly interference for the sake of publicity, that he had a desire to be on the front page every morning, and that his secret ambition was to be Mayor of New York.

Nothing could be farther from the truth. What Thatcher Colt really wanted was to be a musician and poet (in deadly privacy he applied himself to the forms of the sonnet and the villanelle and practiced cadenzas on a flute) but unfortunately nature had made him a detective, and, as he once told me, with that quirkish smile of his, "Not even my duties as Police Commissioner shall keep me from the business of solving crimes."

More than anything else in the world, Thatcher Colt was afraid of being exposed in his true personality as a sentimentalist. He despised all emotion as a weakness, and he got quite angry when I assured him that the cold reason he brought to bear upon his daily work was also an emotion of another kind, a type of orgiastic mental frenzy. I knew him better than he cared to knew himself. He could sit at his desk and deride all human feelings as glandular and depraved, and at that very moment have in his pocket a just-composed sonnet to the red-headed girl who had ditched him for a duke while he was fighting in France. I had known him some years before that disastrous romance, having met him first when I was a reporter on the staff of the old *Sun*. Later, I served under him in the Argonne. But for many years after the demobilization we did not see each other. I had returned to newspaper work and Thatcher Colt was travelling in the Orient. As soon as he came back to New York, he was appointed Police Commissioner and promptly made me his secretary.

All this I recalled at dinner, but as later I hurried through a particularly dank and unpleasant night back to Headquarters, I confess that I was also beguiled with musings about the pretty girl who a few hours before had come to the office with her strange story. Would Thatcher Colt be able to solve the mystery she had laid before him?

In the garage, I found Neil McMahon, the Commissioner's chauffeur, seated at the wheel of that powerful motor car which a great manufacturer recently presented to the Department in gratitude for one of the unpublished exploits of Thatcher Colt. It is an extraordinary machine, equipped with many secret devices from the Triplex non-shatterable glass of its windows and wind-shields to the two concealed sub-caliber Thompson machine guns.

Soon we were joined by the Commissioner, and Neil drove us out into Broome Street. All this part of New York now seemed deserted, and yet within a few minutes walk of us were half of the city's millions, compressed into a

few huddled and jagged tenement streets,—the Italian section around Mulberry Park, and Chinatown, the Bowery
and all the crowded Lower East Side, inhabited chiefly by
Jewish immigrants, made famous in the novels of Fannie
Hurst and Nat Ferber.

His eyes closed, the Commissioner brooded in silence
all through the journey uptown—an exciting journey always with Neil McMahon at the wheel—Neil, who had
four bullet scars from his service in plain clothes, whose
pale, moon face, and faint blue eyes are so inexpressive,
but who blows his siren, goes under the red lights, makes
left-hand passes around street cars, cuts through any maze
of traffic like a knife, and exposes himself and you to
death a dozen times in a simple ride across the town.

Exactly at eight o'clock, Thatcher Colt and I reached the
Esplanade Apartments. The building was one of those archi-
tectural monstrosities which command the high ground
in the region of Columbia University. In the daylight,
from its ornate entrance one can look eastward across the
parked valley at miles of tenements and elevated car tracks,
and beyond these to the river and the long grey ghost of
Hell Gate Bridge. The apartment we sought was in the rear
of the fourth floor, and Betty Canfield opened the door.

"Have you heard anything?" was her first question.

Told that it was too early to hope for any results from
the police inquiries, she at once led us down the tiny
entrance corridor.

The apartment was a pleasant and homelike place with
its two bedrooms, living room, kitchenette and bath. I noticed the gay chintzes, the nice prints, the good-humored
touches of novelty and color in odd and unexpected nooks
and corners. Then I remembered that I was a stranger
intruding here, where one who had waked and slept and
dreamed of her wedding day had gone out and had now
mysteriously disappeared.

Returning to the living room, after roaming from front to back, Thatcher Colt sat down on the edge of the couch and, leaning on his walking stick, shook his head and stared around him with thoughtful eyes as if seeking the truth about Geraldine Foster through clairvoyance. Then he began to question Betty Canfield. Once more I admired the quiet and adroit method which he employed with such consummate skill; he was leading this girl to talk about her friend confidingly, so that she was almost unaware that she was being interrogated by a master of inquisition, dreaded throughout the underworld. For half an hour they chatted on, and at the close Thatcher Colt said:

"I think I have what I want now, Betty—a psychological portrait of Geraldine Foster. A reception clerk in a doctor's office, and why?—Because she wanted to be in the big city, instead of the little town where her parents lived. An ambitious girl who was taking night courses in Columbia University. A good-natured creature—you roomed with her for three years and never had a serious disagreement?"

"That's true," said Betty.

"Loyal to the man she intended to marry," resumed Thatcher Colt, checking off the points of characterization he had drawn forth by his questions. "Sends little presents home to the family every week, although her salary is small and her father is worth perhaps fifty thousand dollars. A girl who is kind to her mother, father, brother. Within three days of her marriage, and poof! she disappears, after that curious conversation you had with her over the telephone."

"Oh, there must be some way of tracing her!" exclaimed Betty, with a quiver of her lovely eyes.

"Easy does it, Betty. I've only just started—and I want to go right on. Mind? Now, this afternoon you referred to your friend's employer, Doctor Humphrey Maskell."

"They call him 'the laughing doctor of Washington Square,'" said Betty, with a toss of her head.

"Who calls him that?"

"His patients and his friends. Geraldine told me."

Thatcher Colt was refilling his pipe.

"Do you think Doctor Maskell has any idea where Geraldine is?" he asked amiably.

"She was quarrelling with him before I called up. And I wouldn't put anything past him. I think I told you his own family won't speak to him."

"Sometimes that is a compliment," said Thatcher Colt, "but not in this instance. There is not a better trial lawyer in New York City than George Maskell. The father is a retired architect, designed the Tablature Building and three or four others—made millions—why, Betty, it's a very fine family."

"All fine families have their dark mutton," declared Betty. "Often Geraldine has sat in that very chair you occupy now and told me about Doctor Maskell and his family. His own brother, George, the lawyer, has not visited him in twenty long years. I think that the doctor did sometimes see his father, but not often. There was a very strange situation in that family. I think Geraldine always had the suspicion that the doctor was a little mad. He was given to unexpected and unexplained absences and he had a mad passion for chopping down trees—he laughs about it and says he is imitating the exiled Kaiser in Doorn and that he loves the swing of the axe."

"But you still haven't told me why the family doesn't like Doctor Maskell?" urged Thatcher Colt.

"I don't know—but I do know that I have always found the personality of the man repelling and I wanted Geraldine to leave him long ago. I believe he could tell us about Geraldine this minute if he chose."

"But that's just a hunch?"

"Of course."

"Maybe it is the doctor who won't have anything to do with the rest of the family—the boot may be on the other foot," suggested Colt. "Anyway, there's nothing so far to confirm your hunch, Betty, or to connect Doctor Maskell with the matter in any way—actually?"

She admitted there was not, and he sat back thoughtfully.

"Betty," he remarked, "I have the impolite feeling that you are not being entirely frank with me about Doctor Maskell."

She flushed slightly.

"I am trying to tell you everything. All that I know is what Geraldine told me. She was very anxious about him. She always said he wasn't as wild as he liked to make out. But she found out last spring that detectives were following the doctor and she always believed his family had employed them."

"George Maskell, you mean?"

"Or Mrs. George, the gorgeous Portia, who made such a hit in the Welkes bad check case. Or even the doctor's father. They are all of them, in spite of their political liberalism, frightened to death that the doctor will do something to disgrace them. He is a fighter when he drinks, you know—but he has been a total abstainer now for several years."

Thatcher Colt smiled with a kind of mild amusement.

"How much our employees know about our private affairs," he remarked.

Betty Canfield flushed with indignation.

"Mr. Colt—"

"Easy, easy," interrupted the Commissioner, "I meant no offense."

"But Geraldine talked to me about her employer because I did not like her working for the doctor—I distrusted him."

"Again—why?"

"Instinctively, as I told you. That feeling led us to talk a good deal about him. Geraldine would come home and tell me how he raved against his own family, because they shut him out—calling his sister-in-law a money-grabbing banshee, making fun of her drawing and singing, and calling his own father a deceived old man. Geraldine used to feel badly about it. And when Mrs. Maskell—the doctor's sister-in-law—went to Europe last summer, I think the doctor tried to make it up with George. But it didn't work and the doctor cursed around the office so that again I tried to make Geraldine resign."

"And she wouldn't?"

"No—she liked him as much as I disliked him." Colt nodded thoughtfully.

"Betty," he said suddenly. "You mentioned that your roommate sometimes stayed away on weekends and holidays."

"Occasionally."

"Did she always confide in you about her personal matters?"

"She used to, but not lately; she often talked with me about the jealousy of Harry Armstrong, her fiancé, for instance, but for the last few months she has grown quite secretive. Ever since she began to talk about having royal blood in her veins."

Thatcher Colt leaned forward.

"What made her say that, Betty?"

"Some one had written to her about her family tree."

"I see. She stopped telling you her secrets then?"

"I don't mean there was any connection. But she did keep her business to herself—most of the time."

"Perhaps you may save her life, you know, by telling everything you know—or suspect."

"I don't know anything. And besides—suppose she were to come back this minute and find me telling you—"

Grotesquely enough there came a ring at the door bell just then. Betty admitted into the living room a well-dressed elderly couple who seemed surprised to find us there. Old Edmund L. Foster, father of the missing girl, was a tall, bent man, with shrewd blue eyes and large, red, gnarled hands which dangled at his sides and gave him a helpless air. His wife was almost as tall as he, but quite stout; her round face was wrinkled and her eyes sparkled excitedly behind double-lensed glasses.

After the introduction, Thatcher Colt explained to the old couple the steps that were being taken to look for their daughter.

"Mr. Colt," pleaded the mother, with an energetic shake of her head, "there won't any of this get into the papers, will there?"

Thatcher Colt explained that if Geraldine continued absent, the help of the press would be invaluable.

"It ruins a girl's reputation to run away," said old Mr. Foster, his voice rumbling in his throat. "And I want you to understand right from the start that Gerry was a good girl. She never got herself into any trouble and never would. There's never been any reflection on our family name, and there never will be."

Thatcher Colt expressed his full confidence in this declaration. He then began interrogating Mr. and Mrs. Foster, and soon was obtaining a verbal picture of the family, their background and history, and all about their former residence in the mountains of Western Maryland, where Mr. Foster had made a substantial fortune in his band instrument factory. Thatcher Colt asked some questions about their son, Bruce, and then inquired why he remained behind at such a time.

"Oh," said Mrs. Foster, with a proud roll of her eyes, "he didn't stay home. Bruce thinks he knows where she is, and he's gone out to look for her himself."

"Where does the young man think she is?" asked the Commissioner quickly.

"We couldn't drag it out of him," explained old Mr. Foster. "He just told us he was going and he wasn't coming back without his sister."

"When was that?"

"This afternoon."

The investigator expressed his thanks for this information.

"Now I would like to have your permission," he said, "to make a search of your daughter's private effects. We might find something—"

"Go ahead," said the father. "You won't find anything to her discredit, I'll promise you that."

The old man and woman sat in two easy chairs, looking at each other but saying nothing at all, while Betty guided the Commissioner in his search, and I, with my note-book followed them.

"Geraldine always used to say she hated the tyranny of things," explained Betty, leading us into the bedroom, "so there isn't much to look at. The new trunk there contains most of her trousseau."

But our search of those garments, scented sweetly for a honeymoon, gave us no information.

"May I see Geraldine's comb?" asked the Commissioner presently. Betty handed him an amber comb which Thatcher Colt looked at with a brief glance of discouragement.

"Not a tiny strand of hair left in it," he remarked disconsolately. "Has she a used hair-net left lying around?"

Betty vanished into a closet and returned with a net cap which she said Geraldine sometimes wore after she had treated her hair. Clinging to it were several strands of fine, brown hair which Thatcher Colt removed with great care. In the breast pocket of his coat he found an envelope into which he dropped the hairs and then sealed the flap. On the outside of the envelope, the Commissioner wrote in his small, precise hand, "Samples of the hair of Geraldine Foster."

Having tucked this in his pocket he turned to a closet door and opened it, revealing a clothes' closet.

"Was this her coat?" asked Thatcher Colt, taking down a tweed jacket, the skirt of which was hanging nearby. As Betty nodded, the Commissioner began fingering through the patch pockets and presently he drew forth a key.

"Is this for your front door?" he asked.

Betty said it was not. Nor did she know what lock it fitted. Thatcher Colt stepped out of the closet and examined the key closely. It was a large one, of greenish metal, with an elliptical bow, a long stem, thick shoulders and a bit composed of a number of irregular projections—a key to fit an intricate and old-fashioned lock. Through the bow was knotted a piece of blue ribbon, as if it had been worn on a loop—perhaps against the bosom of the missing Geraldine.

I put the key in my pocket while Colt asked the parents if they recognized the key. They flatly declared that they did not. With eyes more somber than ever, the Commissioner then resumed his investigation. Betty led the way, pointing out the objects that had belonged to Geraldine.

"We shared this desk—the two left-hand drawers were Geraldine's."

Finding them unlocked, Thatcher Colt removed the drawers and spilled their contents on the couch. Piece by piece he examined the papers, a loose assortment of insurance premium receipts, bills from dry-cleaners and department stores, the commonplace memoranda from any girl's life. Nevertheless, Thatcher Colt asked Betty to preserve them. One letter was found from the father, thanking her for a new necktie. A little later, the Commissioner found a message that had come by special delivery: "Dear Sis, for the love of Mike wire me twenty-five bucks, will you? Your loving brother Bruce." Perhaps there were two hundred separate papers in this disorderly jumble.

"Do you know of any other place where Geraldine might have kept important papers?" asked Thatcher Colt.

"She always boasted she kept only harmless things and destroyed the dangerous ones," replied Betty.

"Everything connected with my daughter was harmless," asserted Edmund L. Foster firmly.

At that moment Thatcher Colt was bending over, on the point of pushing the second drawer of the desk back into place, when suddenly he stopped and thrust his hand and arm deep into the dark recess. Presently he drew out into the light a fragment of green note-paper, on which some words were written in ink. When Thatcher Colt handed the scrap of paper to Betty, she instantly exclaimed:

"That is Geraldine's handwriting,"—and in a low voice she read aloud:

"I will never show the white feather. You tell me it is right. Something tells me it is very wrong. Very wicked. Once in your sleep I heard you utter her name. I am getting married and I need the money. I must have four thousand dollars from you or—"

A deep silence followed her reading of that cryptic fragment of a letter, and especially that last, deeply significant clause. Geraldine Foster a blackmailer? And who had talked in sleep, in the hearing of this pretty girl who could not be found? There was a strange look in the old father's eyes as he kept his gaze fixed on the calm, inscrutable face of his wife—a look of determined, obstinate refusal to believe.

At last Thatcher Colt spoke.

"This is all very different from the mental portrait you gave me of Geraldine," he protested. "The girl you painted for me was not a criminal."

"No! Never!" cried Betty.

The mother and father nodded to each other reassuringly, but said nothing.

"You are sure it is Geraldine's handwriting?" asked Colt.

"Yes. I saw Geraldine when she wrote that note. It was on the morning of Christmas Eve. It was my turn to get breakfast and she was sitting at the desk, writing. All at once she tore up her unfinished letter and threw the pieces into the waste basket. Then she wrote another letter and later mailed it."

"But how does this fragment get way back there, behind the desk drawer?"

For this Betty had no answer, and Thatcher Colt lifted the ornamental waste basket behind the escritoire.

"When did you empty this basket last?" he asked.

"This morning. I am sure those torn-up pieces were still in there—it hadn't been touched since last Saturday."

Thatcher Colt stalked to the telephone, fixed on the wall of the little entrance corridor, and called the switchboard operator in the Esplanade lobby:

"Please tell the janitor to come up to Apartment 4-D at once. Tell him the police want to see him."

While he was waiting, Thatcher Colt stood moodily in the center of the living room, the fragment of paper in his hand, while his eyes studied the inked letters with brooding interest. Familiar with the symptoms of his manner, I watched him eagerly. Something had occurred to him that we had not noticed. Slowly he turned and walked over to the desk, sat down, studied a memorandum Betty had left there, then lifted the desk fountain pen from its swivel holder and began to write on a blank sheet of note-paper lying near his hand.

What he was writing I could not see. It was only a short sentence, and, having put down his pen, he shoved the paper from him, regarded it frowningly, as if expecting it at any moment to become animated and perform a trick for him. Perhaps three minutes of utter silence passed while he watched that piece of paper. Then he lifted it and held it close to his eyes, slanting the paper to an oblique position, looking sharply askance at his own writing, and then comparing it with the torn fragment.

"How long have you been using this kind of ink, Betty?" he asked.

"We have a bottle of it—I think we've had it at least a month."

"Any other ink in the apartment?"

"None that I know of."

Thatcher Colt turned and looked at the girl somberly.

"Think carefully and tell me," he said, "did Geraldine have a special ink bottle of her own?"

"No, sir. Is there anything wrong with that ink?"

Thatcher Colt shrugged.

"I don't know. But I am puzzled at one circumstance. The ink with which I have just written is not the same ink with which Geraldine Foster wrote that note, although both are purple. Geraldine's handwriting seems to me to be in Waterman's ink—certainly it is different from the fluid now in this fountain pen—the metallic glisten of this dried writing of mine shows conclusively that I wrote with what is known as Sheaffer's 'Skrip'—they call it 'washable purple.'"

Without speaking, Betty turned to a closet and came back almost instantly with a bottle of ink in her hand.

"How amazing!" she exclaimed. "That is exactly the name on the label!—Skrip!"

Thatcher Colt smiled grimly.

"That isn't the amazing part," he said. "What is truly extraordinary is that these notes are written in different ink but with the same pen."

"What would that mean, Mr. Colt?"

Before the Commissioner could answer, the door bell rang loudly.

I admitted the janitor, a sleepy Lithuanian in a ragged shirt. Standing in front of the Commissioner his whole body sagged, as if he were sitting on an invisible stool.

"Is today's waste paper still down in the cellar?" asked the Commissioner.

"Tomorrow morning they will take it all away," declared the janitor defensively.

"Then it's still here!" cried Thatcher Colt to me with a sigh of triumph. "Tony, I ordered Sergeant Burke to report to me at my car in front of this house. He ought to be down there now. Show Burke this scrap of torn note, and tell him to go through all the waste paper in the cellar if it takes a week until he finds the rest of the pieces."

With a single electric bulb burning, I left Detective Sergeant Burke seated on a stool in front of two immense bales of waste paper gathered from twelve floors of apartments in the Esplanade. Knowing that this would be, at least, an all-night job, I started back to the apartment on the fourth floor. But I never got there, for I found Thatcher Colt impatiently waiting for me in the lobby. As we hastened out to the sidewalk, I told him that Burke had started on his task. Before we could say more, we were at the Commissioner's car, and Neil McMahon saluted and announced he had something of interest to impart. Neil's actual words were:

"Chief, I got some dirt for you on this Foster case."

"Well?"

"I just got it from the janitor. He was telling me that on or about 8:10 a.m. on the morning of December 24, the said Foster dame and the said Canfield dame were having one hell of a row upstairs. The janitor happened to be in the hallway and he heard it. He don't know what the said girls were fighting about, but he reports that said fight was a lallapaloosa."

"Thanks, Neil. Let's go."

3

THE WOMAN IN THE DARK

Thatcher Colt got into the car and leaning far back he began to fill his pipe. As we started down the shelf-like street that runs along the brink of Morningside, the chief remarked:

"Now, why didn't that charming Betty tell us about that quarrel, Tony? And why didn't she tell us that she was once engaged to Geraldine's brother Bruce?"

"How did you learn that?" I asked quickly.

"From the father, while you were in the cellar. I got some crumbs from him. But he is *not* disposed to be communicative."

I lit a cigarette. We were passing the gaunt and immense edifice of the unfinished Cathedral of St. John the Divine. At our feet lay Manhattan, a lighted garden of brick and steel where millions of people lived. In all those millions, where was Geraldine Foster? I felt saddened inexpressibly; something which I could not single out had suddenly filled me with melancholy.

In silence we drove downtown until we reached the place of our appointment on the north side of Washington Square. The address at which we stopped was almost in the shadow of the triumphal arch which was designed by Stanford White, the victim of Harry Thaw. Oddly, the position of that impressive arch, in the midst of what was once the Potter's Field of Manhattan, is on the very site of the old town gallows.

Doctor Humphrey Maskell had rented the first floor of one of those old-fashioned houses that line the north side of the park, and had made the lower floor into an office suite. As we approached the steps, we saw that a light was burning behind the drawn shades of the office windows. The doctor's brass plate was fixed into the bricks beside the front door. Thatcher Colt and I were about to mount the steps when a figure suddenly appeared in the vestibule. By the light shining through the transom, we saw him clearly, a little man, bent forward as if slightly hunchbacked. His hands were sunk deep into his trousers pockets, his eyes were sliding obliquely and slyly from side to side, as if he were watchful of a sudden attack. As he hesitated a moment, he muttered to himself:

"Get me to talk? Never. Get me to tell? Never. Think I can remember? Never, never, never. But Geraldine was kind to me."

That last phrase—"But Geraldine was kind to me"— seemed to echo in the dark air, as he rushed down the steps and fled past us without a glance. Across the street he hopped, into the parked square, and vanished.

"Now, who do you suppose that was?" I asked.

"I don't know," replied my chief, "but I certainly mean to find out." And as we climbed the marble steps, he added: "He had a face like an ape and yet his eyes were not simian—they were human, and demented!"

Upon ringing, we were promptly admitted into the hallway and found Doctor Maskell in a white linen jacket, standing at the entrance to his offices and smiling affably.

A tall, rather good-looking man was Doctor Humphrey Maskell, broad of shoulder and strong of muscle; a wolf of a man, Thatcher Colt said later. He was in his late thirties, there was a precocious patch of grey in the thick brown hair at his temples, he was recently and exquisitely barbered and his expression was agreeable and yet—or so it seemed to me—with an intangible suggestion of the picaresque. His jaws were set in a long, strong line and his grey eyes were bright and restless.

"Good evening, Mr. Commissioner," he said pleasantly, his voice deep and full. "Will you step in?" and as we followed him into the reception room, he added: "I suppose you want to talk to me about the girl in my office? Yes, certainly," and by that last phrase Doctor Maskell answered his question for himself.

The doors of the suite were thrown open so that we could see the lay-out of the rooms at once. The front room was furnished with many chairs for waiting patients, a table heaped with magazines, and a few etchings on the papered walls. A partition separated this from the doctor's private consultation room, in which I made out a desk, an examination table in white enamel, a light-ray apparatus and other therapeutic paraphernalia. Beyond this was a closed door which, as we learned later, opened into a small storage room at the back, with a window looking upon the rear yard of the house.

The doctor invited us to be seated, lit a cigarette, and waited for Thatcher Colt to speak.

"Forgive me for an abrupt beginning," said the Commissioner, "but did some one just leave here as we entered?"

"Yes, certainly," replied Doctor Maskell, in his deep voice. "A poor misshapen child who might have been left on my door-step by the fairies. He is a combination valet and chauffeur and cook for a lonely bachelor like myself. His name is Checkles."

"Checkles?"

"Yes, certainly—Checkles. I brought him home from the war, which broke his body and his mind, and left him an oaf who knew nothing more than to cry and run at the nose. I am gradually giving him a new body and a new mind."

Thatcher Colt had inclined his head forward as if he were studying the physician's knees.

"I remember you in the war," he said in a low voice. "They called you the 'fighting doctor.'"

Humphrey Maskell laughed.

"Yes, certainly," he agreed.

"Tell me what you know about the disappearance of Miss Foster," suggested Thatcher Colt, abruptly.

"I don't know anything about it at all," replied Doctor Maskell in a reasoning tone. "I wish I did. Geraldine was going to leave me to be married, but this sudden and unexplained absence makes me feel quite alarmed."

"When did you last see her?" asked Thatcher Colt, leaning forward on his stick and peering around the room.

"At two o'clock on Saturday afternoon, Christmas Eve."

"Two o'clock, did you say?" asked Thatcher Colt with sudden interest.

"Yes."

"How was that?"

"Well, I shall have to explain to you that every year I make a practice of giving presents to my regular patients. I like to deliver them in person, the day before Christmas. Last week, I observed that custom. All during Saturday morning, Geraldine was here in the office, helping me wrap the bundles and attach the cards. Around noon she went out to lunch, but she came back a few minutes after one. She helped me load the first batch of presents into my car and I drove off."

"Was she with you?"

"No," replied the doctor with a broad smile. "I had another lady with me. She was Miss Doris Morgan, a little girl eleven years old, who lives with her mother and father and grandmother on the floor above these offices. She came with me to help distribute the little presents. We called it playing Santa Claus."

"What time did you get back here?"

"About 1:45 I should judge. We drove to about a dozen houses in the Village district and then we came back for more presents."

Thatcher Colt nodded, closed his eyes, and leaned back against the wall.

"You filled your car with more presents then?"

"Yes."

"And when did you leave on your second trip?"

"At two o'clock. And that was the last time I saw Geraldine Foster."

Thatcher Colt's eyes closed even more tightly and he smoked for a moment in silence.

"Now, Doctor," he said evenly, "let me get this picture straight in my mind. You left this office for your second trip at two o'clock on the afternoon of December 24?"

"Yes, certainly. But why all these questions about—"

"Where did you go on that second trip?"

"All over town."

"And when did you get back?"

"Oh, it was dark. Well after four o'clock—nearly five, I should say."

Again Thatcher Colt closed his eyes.

"What happened when you came home?" he asked.

"Mr. Colt," said the physician, "a very remarkable thing happened when I came home. I am sure it could have no bearing on this matter. Yet I suppose I ought to tell you."

Thatcher Colt opened his eyes and studied the doctor calmly.

"Better tell me everything," he said dryly.

"I was holding Doris by the hand, and we were both laughing, as I came through the front door into the hallway out there, just outside the door to this office. But as I stepped into the hallway, I noticed a woman standing in front of my office door. The hall-lamp was not burning and I could see her only indistinctly. But I did make out that she was dressed in a dark coat, with the collar turned up, and that she stood so that her face was turned away from us. I spoke to her and asked her if she wanted to see the doctor. She answered me by demanding to know why I did not keep some one in the office while I was away. I said there was a young lady inside and the strange woman then insisted that she had been ringing for fifteen minutes and yet no one had opened the door. I thought this was very peculiar, for Geraldine was always most faithful and punctual about her duties. I tried the door and to my surprise it was locked. I opened the door with my key and walked in. Doris followed me and so, without a word, did this woman. There were no lights on in my office and I called out for Geraldine. No answer. Then, to my astonishment, the strange woman pushed past me, without asking my permission, and walked straight through this reception room, into my consultation room yonder. Of course I followed her, but before I reached her side, she had gone on farther and opened the rear door and looked into the little room at the back. That, too, was empty. I then asked her, rather peremptorily, what she was looking for, but she buried her chin in the collar of her coat, half-closed her eyes and said she was too late. Then she burst into tears. I tried to detain her, but she rushed past me, out into the hallway. I followed her, quite startled at her extraordinary behavior, and then I noticed there was a taxicab before my door. She got into it and drove away."

"You didn't notice the license number on the taxi, I suppose?" asked Thatcher Colt.

Doctor Maskell had not.

"And that," said Doctor Maskell soberly, "is all that I know about it. At first I was inclined to think that Geraldine had played me a rather shabby trick—recently she has not been herself; talked about having royal blood in her veins—but now, I confess, I don't know what to think."

"You have no idea who the woman was?"

"No."

"Was she young or old?"

"I had the impression that she was around middle age."

"It could not have been Geraldine herself?"

"Good Lord, no!"

Thatcher Colt emptied the dottie from his pipe into an ash-tray and began refilling the bowl.

"Queer," he said musingly. "That mysterious lady might have been just a wandering person with a disorderly mind. On the other hand, she may yet prove to be of supreme importance in this case."

"Yes, certainly," agreed Doctor Maskell.

"I shall take a look through your establishment. Mind?" asked Thatcher Colt.

"Do you think Geraldine is still here?" asked the doctor, opening wide his eyes.

Without answering, the Police Commissioner rose and strode through the two rooms to the door at the back and through that into the rear room. I followed him, with Doctor Maskell marching at my heels. The somber, brown eyes of Thatcher Colt were turning from one object to another in the clutter of stored material in that last room of the suite. Bending down, he fingered bottles and packages that lay loosely around and I noticed that over one large bottle he lingered. Stolidly the doctor watched as the Commissioner removed the stout cork, and sniffed at the neck of the bottle. Then, still without a word, Thatcher

Colt left the bottle and went on prowling into the consultation room. He halted suddenly before a closed door.

"What is that?"

"A clothes' closet," answered Doctor Maskell.

Thatcher Colt opened it and thrust his hand inside.

"May I ask," inquired Maskell, "what you hope to find in there, Mr. Commissioner?"

Backing out of the closet, Thatcher Colt showed a brown fur coat in his hand.

"Did this belong to Geraldine Poster?" he asked, turning toward the doctor and staring at him with profound melancholy.

"Yes, certainly. I cannot imagine what it is doing in there. I did not know it was there. The closet has not been opened by me since Saturday."

"Was this the coat she wore to work on Christmas Eve?"

"I am certain that it was. I saw her with it on when she went out to lunch."

Thatcher Colt closed his eyes as he stood there with the girl's coat held against his chest.

"Christmas Eve was a cold day," he said in a low voice. "The air was damp and raw and piercing. If Geraldine were going out anywhere, she would need her coat. And there is her bag, hanging on the same nail with her coat. Where can the owner be—if she went out with no coat and no purse?"

In a strained silence we stood there while Thatcher Colt examined the purse, checking up on the small miscellany of its contents,—compact, lipstick, a book of addresses, a roll of bills and a handful of silver. Putting the coat and bag into my hands, the Commissioner turned again to Doctor Maskell.

"Do you suppose the mysterious woman who accosted you brought back the coat and purse? Did you notice if she carried anything?"

"Why—why—no, I did not," answered the physician. "What makes you think about that?"

"I am sorry if I have inconvenienced you," replied Thatcher Colt gloomily. "And I am sorry to say that I may have to trouble you soon again. For the present, good-night."

"Yes, certainly," said Doctor Maskell, opening wide his door and bowing.

But at the threshold, Thatcher Colt paused.

"Doctor," he said, "I am sorry to observe, on departing, that you have not been frank with me."

"What do you mean?" returned Maskell sharply.

"You failed to tell me that you and Geraldine quarreled before you left on your errand of good cheer. You had a beastly quarrel, but you have kept quiet about it."

Doctor Maskell looked startled, then shrugged his shoulders.

"That is true," he admitted. "But it was a private matter. If Miss Foster returns, she will not want me to discuss the subject."

"But the police do want you to discuss it. What did you quarrel about?"

Again the physician shrugged his shoulders helplessly.

"About her engagement. She had broken it off. She told me about it. I told her she was a fool—that she should go through with the marriage. That is why we quarreled."

"Why did she say she had broken off the engagement?"

"She did not tell me that."

The doctor was lying. Thatcher Colt knew that he was lying, and Maskell knew that he knew.

Without a word, the Commissioner turned his back on the physician and I followed him out into the vestibule. Behind us the door of the Maskell offices closed quietly but with a click that told us also how securely it was shut against us.

4

WHO IS EPHRAIM?

I had started down the white marble steps of the house on Washington Square, North, when I was suddenly halted by a brief, tense word from Thatcher Colt. Looking back, I saw that he was standing in the vestibule, his pocket electric torch playing over the name-plates beside the door bells. As I returned to his side, he was pressing a button near the name "Gilbert Morgan".

Presently the familiar clicking of the latch was heard and once again the front door yielded to my hand on the knob. Up the broad staircase I followed my chief, to the second floor, where we found a woman standing at an open door, her face in shadow, but her blonde hair was radiant in the fall of yellow light from a lamp suspended above and behind her head.

"Is this Mrs. Morgan?" asked Colt promptly.

Without immediately replying, the woman looked at him closely and meanwhile I studied her. In spite of all that has since been said against her, I have always maintained that Mrs. Morgan was a beautiful woman. Odd as this may sound to those who know the history of the case, I nevertheless mean beautiful in its finest sense. There was more than prettiness to her soft and gentle features, and the tragic restlessness of her large and lustrous blue eyes. She was a young woman, and, I repeat it, beautiful, but there was a lifetime of suffering in the watchful eyes, in the very tone with which she greeted us.

"I am Felise Morgan," she replied. "What is it you wish?"

Briefly and naturally, Thatcher Colt explained who he was and why he was there. But at the very mention of Geraldine Foster's name a gleam flashed dangerously from the woman's blue eyes.

"I know nothing about Geraldine Foster," she answered firmly.

Making no comment upon the evident spirit with which this statement was made, Thatcher Colt repeated to her the story that had just been told to him by Doctor Maskell. To all its details Mrs. Morgan nodded confirmingly. It was true that her little daughter, Doris, had helped the doctor with the distribution of his Christmas presents. It was true that they had been gone on their trip about the length of time fixed by Maskell.

"Might we talk to your daughter?" suggested Colt.

"She is asleep," protested the mother, upon which Thatcher Colt waved his hand, dismissing the notion. But Mrs. Morgan agreed that Thatcher Colt might question the little girl, if it ever became necessary, unless her father objected. Mr. Morgan was not then at home.

For the second time that night, we left the house and returned to the street. There were a dozen questions clamoring in my mind, but the mood of Thatcher Colt forbade any inquiry just then.

"A lioness of a woman, that Felise Morgan," was his only comment.

Indeed, when his mind is working on a problem in crime, Thatcher Colt is never a talkative man. All the way to Headquarters he was silent and contemplative, smoking his pipe as he lounged back in the car. Centre Street was deserted when we reached the grim old Department building, with its marble trim and its ornamental iron, very

massive and Georgian in the December night. I was glad
to get inside, for there was a raw, pneumonia wind abroad.
As we walked through the vaulted stone corridors, past
the marble tablets carved with the names of policemen
and detectives who died in the performance of their duty,
our footsteps echoed on the resounding flagstones. Still
Thatcher Colt remained silent, but the very atmosphere
of the old building, a place of badges, raincoats, billies,
caps and handcuffs, seemed to charge him with new life.
No Commissioner ever loved the Department with more
ardent or fanatical interest.

On his desk lay a stack of reports and he began to finger
them swiftly—accounts of what was going forward in the
police work of many divisions, the boiler, the bomb, the
safe and loft squads, the Bureau of Crime Prevention—he
gathered their import with acquisitive eyes.

From a mass of these documents he picked up a lay-out
for a police circular, prepared by Captain Laird, to broad-
cast the search for Geraldine Foster. It was ready to go to
the printer, and a few days later was being displayed all
over the country. With a pencil, Thatcher Colt made a few
swift corrections.

Then, while I spread out on a table the long key with
its knot of blue ribbon, the letters, the coat and the purse
that belonged to Geraldine Foster, all of which would be
turned over to the Headquarters' property clerk, the Commissioner continued to read quickly through a sheaf of
notes left for him by Captain Henry.

"Laird has found nothing," he said glumly. "And Burke
telephoned he had plowed through the first waste paper
bale and had found none of the missing pieces. But I will
put a tail on Doctor Maskell—that may help"—by which
the Commissioner meant he would have Maskell followed,
night and day.

I sat down at the typewriter and began to transcribe my notes. In my book, I had complete records of all that had been told us by Betty Canfield, the Fosters, Mrs. Morgan and Doctor Humphrey Maskell. As I reduced the pothooks to typewritten sheets, it seemed to me—though, God knows, with no sense of disloyalty—that all of Thatcher Colt's questions, his groping for evidence and witnesses had led him only into an increasing mystery and darkness, instead of nearer to the light.

By noon of the following day, there was still no word of Geraldine Foster. Thatcher Colt had spent most of the morning at the Police College across the street from Headquarters. There he had delivered his famous physical training lecture which no "rookie" ever forgets—inspiring the students with a desire to learn how to "get their man"—the scientific way of handling bullies and ruffians, the important holds in jiu-jitsu, in which Colt is an expert, and similar mysteries. Not all of his morning, however, was spent in the college. While waiting for his first caller, he explained to me that he had done some solitary prowling in Washington Square, just after breakfast, and had learned two interesting facts.

"I talked with a girl named Lizzie Clark," he explained, with a glint of amusing reminiscence in his eye. "She is a nurse-maid for an Italian family living in the Fifth Avenue Hotel. Lizzie remembers seeing two women leave the house, where Maskell has his office, on the afternoon of Christmas Eve. What fixed it in her mind was that each of the women carried a large bottle, almost the size of a jug."

"Can you be certain one of them was Geraldine Foster?" I inquired.

"No," admitted the Commissioner, with a sigh. "But there was a large jug-like bottle in Maskell's office last night—and near it some wrapping paper with a tag, showing three bottles to be delivered before three p.m. on Christmas Eve."

He spoke lightly and yet I could tell there was a worried note in his voice.

"Also," added the Commissioner, "Doctor Maskell has left town."

"Where on earth—"

"Right you are! Where on earth? Checkles doesn't know. No one seems to know. The smiling doctor of Washington Square has decamped. He eluded my man, an hour after he began to tail him. But why shouldn't he go away? There are no charges against him."

I was alert to ask for more details, but Captain Laird arrived and I went back to my notes.

The chief of the Bureau of Missing Persons promptly stated, as his theory, that the girl was alive and in deliberate hiding. He pointed out that she had remained away before for days at a time.

"So far, it is just like any one of a number of such cases," argued Captain Laird. "We have them all the time. I am certain the girl will return."

"I hope you are right," said the chief emphatically. "But there are elements in this disappearance which make me skeptical—her remarks over the telephone and in that fragment of a note—also the curious mystery of the fur coat and the purse. And now Maskell has run out on us. Makes me remember other cases that were not so simple, Captain. You remember Alice Corbett?"

Captain Laird remembered her. On Friday, November 13, 1925, Alice Corbett, a junior student, vanished from Smith College, in Northampton, Massachusetts.

"Do you recall the laconic and singular message that she left?" persisted Thatcher Colt. "'Mother, I am going home', she wrote in her note. And that was the last that was ever heard of her."

"Nevertheless, I have always believed Alice Corbett to be still alive," argued Laird.

"That's what people also believed about Frances St. John Smith," returned the Commissioner. "Frances disappeared from the same college as Alice Corbett, and oddly enough, also, on Friday, the thirteenth. There was the mystery of a pretty girl, only eighteen years old, talented and worth a million dollars or more—it was months before they found her dead body floating in a pond. What happened? We don't know, any more than we know the fate of Dorothy Arnold, or, more recently, what befell the beautiful Mrs. McDowell Rogers when last year she vanished from Barrington Manor in Louisville, Kentucky, apparently never to return. I tell you, the unexplained absence of a beautiful girl is, to me, a danger signal. It has always been so, ever since Elsie Sigel was chopped up and packed into a Chinaman's trunk. We must find Geraldine Foster, dead or alive."

Just then, Captain Henry came in, saluted, and announced that Sergeant Burke wanted to talk to the Commissioner.

"Bring him in at once."

Burke marched into the office, his hat in his hand. The detective's face was red and his eyes were rolling.

"I have the honor to report that I have been through all the bales and I have not found the missing pieces, Mr. Commissioner," he said lugubriously.

Thatcher Colt glared at the detective.

"And you call yourself a detective, Burke?"

To our surprise, Burke replied by laying a handful of green paper fragments before the Commissioner.

"What's this, Burke? You just told me you couldn't find them."

"I couldn't, Sir," pleaded the distressed detective. "But I found these instead. They are pieces of a note written by the Foster girl—but they don't belong to the piece you showed me."

Hastily, Thatcher Colt fitted the pieces together and read the letter aloud:

"Dear Harry,—
"After what has happened, I can never marry you. This is the end of it. You could not love me and take the position you do. I love you—the you I knew before—but I shall never see you again.
"Geraldine."

For a moment, there was a complete silence in the Commissioner's office. At length it was broken by Captain Laird.

"Who is Harry?" he asked.

"Harry Armstrong—the boy she was to marry, of course. This is odd! Did she tear up two letters—where in God's name are the missing pieces of the other one?"

Burke held up his right hand as if taking the oath and avouched that he had personally examined every single scrap.

"Go back and try again!" said Thatcher Colt, and Burke, rolling his eyes until only the whites could be seen, departed from the office. As Captain Laird and I stood beside the desk, the Commissioner leaned over the torn pieces of paper and said:

"Don't you see that this note is written with the household ink used in the girls' apartment—this makes the other note—the blackmail one—even more curious. I wonder if I have sent Burke on a wild goose chase?"

In fact, he had, as the offended Burke will continue to tell to his grand-children. Indeed, the whole, nation-wide quest for the missing Geraldine seemed to be fruitless, as day followed day without results. Seven times, during those busy days, Geraldine Foster was reported found, but all were frauds. Such disappointments are an inevitable part of all such girl-hunts, for no fair-seeming clue can be ignored.

But Thatcher Colt, at times neglecting other important duties, stuck to the case. What clues there were seemed inadequate and confusing. There was, for example, what Thatcher Colt referred to as the "Clue of Ephraim Foster". This was unearthed in some of the letters which Geraldine had written home and which the Commissioner studied with great care. Among them, he found the reason why Geraldine had taken to telling her friends she had royal blood in her veins. She had got the idea from letters written to her by one Ephraim Foster, of Willoughby, Kansas. This Mr. Foster was tracing the genealogical history of the Foster family, writing to every one by the name of Foster he could find and intended to write a book on the subject.

"We come from the groins of kings," wrote the old gentleman to Geraldine, in a letter which the girl had sent proudly home to her parents.

I greatly admired the precision and despatch with which Colt acted on that seemingly trivial due. He called six detective sergeants into his office, read them the letter and showed them the open pages of a telephone book.

"Divide up the Fosters among yourselves," ordered Colt. "Call on them and find out how many received similar letters."

By five o'clock the next afternoon, we knew that none of the several hundred Fosters living in New York had received such a letter. Apparently the ancestor-enthusiast, Ephraim Foster, had written only to the girl who now could not be found. A set expression was in my chief's eyes as he dictated a wire to the Chief of Police of Willoughby, Kansas, asking for information about Ephraim Foster.

I remember that I sent that telegram on the night of January 6. The reply that came the following morning greatly astonished us:

"Ephraim Foster had post-office box here last summer. Understand not a man but a woman. Did not live in town but drove in from some other town to get her mail. Anything we can do?

"Chief of Police Dewyre."

Keenly aroused by this unexpected development, Thatcher Colt wired him to follow any trace as far as possible. While he realized that this might have no relation to the disappearance, it looked sufficiently peculiar to follow through. But before we had heard again from the West, there came a new development that drove all other matters temporarily from our minds.

This new development was the finding of the fragments of the second—which I have called the blackmail—note of Geraldine Foster. It was just at the noon hour of January 7, Betty Canfield called the office and talked to Thatcher Colt. Presently he turned from the telephone, his face glowing with excitement.

"Betty Canfield has found the missing pieces of that note. They were behind the desk drawer," he exclaimed. "Funny—I looked there, too. Get on the telephone extension, Tony, and take down the contents of the message in shorthand while she reads it to me."

Two second later, I was listening in and copying down the following:

"My dear Casanova:—
"There is nothing you can do about it. If I tell, your happiness will be destroyed. What is the small amount I need compared with your happiness? I think I am letting you off very easily. Particularly as I do not approve of your romance and cannot be scared by your

threats. I will never show the white feather.
You tell me it is right. Something tells me
it is very wrong. Very wicked. Once in your
sleep I heard you utter her name. I am getting married and I need the money. I must
have four thousand dollars from you or I will
tell about the house on Peddler's Road. Thank
God I have—"

There, Betty told us, the note abruptly finished.

Instantly saying good-bye to her, with a promise that he
would send for her later, Colt turned from the regulation
to the inter-office telephone. To another division of that
immense department which he loved to call the "Standing
Army of the City of New York," he put a question:

"Helloa—Brampton? Is there such a place in the five
boroughs anywhere as Peddler's Road? What? All right, I'll
hold on."

He turned and looked somberly at me.

"That note sounds bad," he said. "Who was Casanova?"

Then he spoke again into the 'phone and listened to
the crisp voice, giving directions from the other end.

"Thanks," said Thatcher Colt finally, and turned to me
as he replaced the receiver.

I knew what my chief would do. He would telephone to
the Precinct Captain in the neighborhood, wherever Peddler's Road might lie and give his instructions. The Precinct Captain would "turn on the light". The patrolman
on the beat, within ten or fifteen minutes, would be near
the patrol-box and observe the signal light flashing. He
would telephone to the station-house and be told to find
out what he could about the houses on Peddler's Road.

"Chief," I said, "I wish you would let me do that job.
I'm all up on my work here."

Thatcher Colt smiled.

"All right," he said, "Peddler's Road is on Manhattan Island, although I confess I have never heard of it before. Brampton tells me it is a small lane, running across some undeveloped property behind Riverside Drive near the Dyckman Street ferry up on the hill there, near the Rockefeller property. I don't know that there is much chance of finding anything important, but you could hop up there right off and take a look around. Mind? This note says the 'house on Peddler's Road' and Brampton says it is just a block in length, so you won't have far to look. Report right back here—Captain Laird and I are having lunch to talk over the case."

I was already in my overcoat and on my way.

But here I must confess to an act of mine which may have seemed like carelessness. There was no intention of disloyalty on my part whatever, but it did not seem to me then that an hour's time would make an important difference. The fact was that in the morning I had telephoned Betty Canfield at the Esplanade Apartments and invited her to lunch with me to discuss the disappearance of her friend. I did not think it necessary to break the engagement in order to carry out instructions—an hour or so either way would make no difference.

Accordingly I met Betty at a Portuguese restaurant on Broad Street and I found her a very charming luncheon companion. Of course we talked about the fragments of the note she had found, but at first I tried to avoid a discussion of the case. Instead, I got her to tell me about herself, and listened with growing interest as she related incidents of her childhood down in their Western Maryland home. Her family still lived in Wingsboro, a little mountain town, where they had been neighbors of the Fosters. Betty and Geraldine had come to New York about the same time. Geraldine was studying night courses in accountancy while Betty was learning interior decoration in which she was now highly successful, having a good position with a firm on Madison Avenue. At no time did Betty refer to her engagement to Bruce Foster, the brother of the missing girl, and I did not have the effrontery to ask her about it, much as I wished to know if it still existed. Presently she asked me to tell her about my work, which I did, quite willingly, and we lingered over the table while I talked authoritatively of the police department and my devotion to Thatcher Colt.

"I think you are a good detective yourself," smiled Betty. "But I suppose that comes from your newspaper training."

"How did you know I was a reporter?" I asked. She laughed.

"I know more than that," she said. "You were in the war and served with your old friend, the Commissioner, and you were never afraid of anybody but him, and the only thing you want in the world is another war, and I hope you never get it, and you're proud of your drinking capacity, aren't you?"

I stared across at her in amazement.

"You must be a detective yourself," I stammered. "Who told you all that about me?"

But she only laughed and said she always liked to know something in advance about people with whom she had lunch. I saw then that she had talked with Thatcher Colt when I was not present.

Then Betty begged me to tell her more about what Thatcher Colt was doing to find her roommate. So interested was she in the search that I then and there confided to her my assignment, whereupon she pleaded to let her accompany me uptown.

In this request, I saw no real harm. Betty's interest in the case was so keen, and her knowledge of Geraldine Foster so valuable that I was glad to have her. It was about half-past two o'clock when I telephoned for a department car and we started our long drive from the lower part of the Island into Upper Manhattan near the frontier line of the Harlem River.

At Dyckman Street we left the car and after some search climbed a narrow path that started from Broadway and toiled up a steep slope into a region strangely at variance with the built-up streets that hemmed it all around. Like an oasis of forgotten country, this stretch of land hid itself in the midst of a region filled with apartment houses, stores and garages, with the ferry slip and the river only a few thousand feet away. Old trees were growing there, and a few quaint and abandoned frame houses, now falling to pieces.

I remember that as we trudged forward up the hill, a small sallow-faced boy passed us and I called to him, "Where is Peddler's Road?"

He opened his mouth, showing his buck teeth, and said:

"Up there by the haunted house where you can see the naked ghost."

"What's that? Come here!" I cried, but the boy ran down the steep slope, and was almost instantly lost to sight. Betty and I looked at each other and then laughed, for the encounter then seemed odd and yet absurd, and our own lost situation somewhat ridiculous. Was this lane which now had led us to the heights of this promontory the Peddler's Road that we had come here to seek? There seemed no way of telling, in this disarray of bare trees, frozen sod and rutted by-path, set down in the midst of a great city—this mountain wilderness where there were no street signs, guide posts, nor the sight of any living human being of whom we might inquire.

"I think this must be the place," said Betty, pointing to a turn into a wider sort of road, but in no better condition, a few feet beyond. There were a few large old trees,

whose bare boughs scraped and cried in the wind of that
blear afternoon, and skirting these we came suddenly upon
a lonely house—the only dwelling on what we learned
later was really Peddler's Road.

What we had come upon was a two-story wooden
house, called a portable, or assembled house, manufac-
tured in sections and often sold through the mail. This
was a charming one, in good condition, newly painted
white with green windows and door sills. Its green pitch
roof and the white scrim curtains produced a pleasing and
home-like impression.

"Perhaps," I said, "there is some one home, and we can
make inquiries. But first, let's take a look around."

Leading the way, I passed to the rear of the house,
where at first I found nothing unusual, except one broken
kitchen window. I detected no signs of life, but instead, in
the next minute, I came upon startling evidence of death.

Seven pigeons lay dead on the ground almost at my feet.
Such a collection of dead birds was sufficiently unusual
to make me stop and look more closely and, while Betty
turned away, I picked up one of the pigeons, only to let it
fall in sudden dismay; what I had seen had greatly startled me—the breast feathers of the dead bird were smeared
with red; a scarlet splash against the white breast of the
dead creature. The next moment, regretting my weakness,
I picked it up and examined it more closely wondering
if some one had been heartless enough to kill all these
pigeons out of sheer wantonness. But I could find no
wound upon the bird, nor any evidence of violence. One
after another, I took the remaining birds into my hands,
only to find the same scarlet daubs upon their feathers,
and no signs of injury.

"I am sorry, Betty," I said, "but all this is very peculiar.
What are these red stains on the poor birds? Have they
been drinking red paint and poisoned themselves or—"

I stopped, struck with a fantastic notion. Those stains on the breast—could they be blood stains? How had they come there? Was there some open stream near by where the pigeons flew to drink? Had they drunk from a brook that ran red with human blood?

Then I told myself that my mind was making up horror tales. Yet the feeling persisted and it was with deep misgivings I left the birds and followed Betty to the front of the house, and without another word rapped on the door. There was no answer, although I knocked repeatedly. Fantastic fears filled my mind—but I told myself they were probably unreasonable. Why should the sight of those dead pigeons so stir up my imagination? Again and again I knocked upon the door but without result, and finally I impatiently tried the knob. To my surprise, it yielded and the door opened at a slight push of my hand.

I stepped inside and then stood, arrested and appalled, rooted at the threshold. My first glance around the living room into which I had walked told me that a horrible crime had been committed there. Everything seemed bedaubed with blood. I have never seen such a spectacle of fury let loose within four walls. Tables, chairs, book-cases all were flung around, topsy-turvy and helter-skelter, as if overturned in some life and death struggle. Even in the shadows, I could see that blood was smeared everywhere, staining the drapes, spotting the walls and slopped and clotted in dried patches on the floor.

"For God's sake, don't come in here, Betty," I called.

I glanced over my shoulder and got a glimpse of her drawn and frightened face. She had seen, and now she stood there in the winter sunlight with her gloved hands lifted against her cheeks and her eyes closing with fear. Then I turned back to the room. My hand was groping for an electric switch-button when I suddenly stopped.

I heard a noise—the sound of a footstep on the stairs. Only a slight and inconsequential sound it was, merely the scraping of a shoe. But it was the sound of something moving and alive in this house where murder, fell, barbarous and hideous, had recently been committed.

Had I been mistaken? Was the noise only the delusion of an over-wrought imagination? But no—the sound came again. There were certainly footsteps descending a staircase into this very room.

I drew my revolver and waited. Then, suddenly I heard a well-remembered voice, yet sharpened with an unfamiliar choler.

"Put down your gun," said the voice. "It is a fancy weapon, I see, a Smith and Wesson, .38 caliber, blue steel and four-inch barrel. And I suppose you took it from a pocket holster with the fastest draw and surest lock. All very impressive to the young lady. But you won't shoot. You're no cop—you're too busy taking girls to lunch to be a policeman."

I put down the gun and stood, shame-faced and guilty as Thatcher Colt walked into the room.

5

TWILIGHT ON PEDDLER'S ROAD

As the Police Commissioner pressed a button, the lights in the wall bracket lamps glowed softly over the shocking confusion of the room. But I had no eyes, then, for these evidences of ferocity. Instead, I looked at Thatcher Colt, wondering how and why he was here.

"Tony," he said, "I caught an accidental glimpse of you and your lady friend at luncheon. While you were chatting over a table with a girl, I came up here and made the discovery that could have been yours—and would have made you a reputation."

"I'm sorry, Chief, I—"

He waved aside my contrition.

"The girl we have been looking for was most probably murdered in this room. You remember that I carried away from her apartment a sample of her hair? Well, in this room I have found other samples—soaked with blood, true, but from the same head, I feel convinced. I found them clinging to the blade of this."

From the shadows of a corner behind him there, Thatcher Colt lifted an ugly implement—an axe with a short handle, a double-bitted affair that gleamed in the light. On the steel blade were dark red stains. You will find that axe today, exposed in a glass case, in the Crime Museum that is on the sixth floor of the Police College, across the street from Police Headquarters in what was once the Loft candy factory. There, between the exhibits in the Snyder-Gray murder and the affair of the assassinated physician, repose the relics in the Geraldine Foster mystery—among them a pillow case, a half-finished note of green paper, pieced together with tissue paper, three envelopes of human hair, and this axe. On its bit the blood of the victim is still thick and crusted, just as when Thatcher Colt found it that dreary winter's afternoon.

"Good God!" I said involuntarily, as Thatcher Colt swung the axe above his head until it whistled through the air.

"Geraldine Foster has been hacked to death," he said somberly. "Somewhere near this house we shall find her body—buried, because I found a garden spade in the kitchen, apparently used quite lately. The murderer wore silk gloves, leaving thumb and finger prints on the handle of both the axe and the spade, but no loops, no whorls, no real identification. Moreover, the person who committed this crime was five feet, eleven inches tall, exceptionally strong."

I gazed at my chief, amazed.

"That is clear to me because once the axe blade in a particularly vicious swing struck the wall—the mark over there is plain—we can at least guess at the height from that."

As he talked, he kept nodding his head and looking from one corner to another.

"Moreover," he said, "the lock on the front door has recently been repaired, the kitchen window broken, and the house burglarized through the broken window—either by a midget or a small boy. The footprints in the dust show that much. Further, Tony, the house has had some feather burglars. Since the kitchen window glass was smashed, pigeons have taken to roosting within these walls—they even drank of warm human blood, and then, struggling to get into the open air, they died. One could not make it—I found the little corpse in the kitchen."

"It is extraordinary how you can know these things," I gasped.

Thatcher Colt's eyes were still roaming stealthily around the room.

"There is much more to be learned," he replied irritably. "I am inclined to believe that a boy with a sallow face and buck teeth actually saw a part, at least, of the murder. But he thinks he saw a ghost. Fortunately I have his name and address. I didn't have time to stop then and question him fully."

What a bungler Thatcher Colt would justly have thought me, if I had told him the truth—how the same boy had crossed my path, and I had let him run off. But of this I said nothing until long afterward.

While he was talking, the Commissioner was prowling and roaming back and forth, bending to examine the edge of a table, even the rungs in the back of a chair.

Suddenly I heard him give a low whistle and drop to his knees. From the floor he lifted what seemed to be a hair or else a thin strand of some fabric, about four inches long.

"Just a straw, Tony," he said. "A straw to show the way the wind blows. A piece of human hair—golden hair—that might belong to some innocent person—yet which might have dropped from the head of the murderer."

From his pocket, he produced one of his inevitable blank envelopes, put the hair carefully away and marked it on the outside for future identification.

"The brutality of this crime," he informed me, "is the best promise of its solution. I am already convinced that the method employed was not the adventitious result of sudden fury; it was neither casual nor accidental. This deed was planned. I knew that after I had walked up the stairs. The bathroom smelt strangely of the bark of pine trees. When we find out why, Tony, I fancy we shall unearth a peculiar fiendishness behind this murder."

Suddenly the door knob rattled and the front door was pushed open without ceremony. Thatcher Colt sprang around and we both faced the entrance only to find Betty Canfield staring in at us. She looked pale and ill.

"Chief, it's all my fault," I pleaded. "May we send Miss Canfield home?"

"In the investigation of a suspicious death," he said sarcastically, "it is the duty of the police to prevent unauthorized persons from entering upon the scene of a crime until a member of the Detective Division appears. All that is clearly set forth in the Manual of Police Procedure and Practice. But it is also stated in that excellent treatise that it is essential for a proper identification of the body of the deceased to be made. Now, under the one rule, I can't admit you in the house, Betty, but under the other I must ask you to remain nearby."

His words and manner seemed unnecessarily harsh to me, and yet I could appreciate how he resented my lingering to lunch with Betty when I should have obeyed his instructions to the letter.

"All right," said Betty. "I shall wait outside until you call me."

"One moment," said Thatcher Colt, and striding toward her, held out his hand. On his palm, he laid an object wrapped in a handkerchief, and as he drew back the folds, I saw that it was a platinum wrist watch.

"It's Geraldine's," ejaculated Betty, with a low gasp.

"Observe," said Thatcher Colt, "that the crystal is broken, and the hands and case dented. It was undoubtedly struck by one of those blows with the axe. If they have not been tampered with or moved, the hands indicate the hour of death—5:10 p.m."

"Where did you find it, Mr. Colt?" asked Betty, with a piteous glance at me.

"In the bath-tub," answered Thatcher Colt.

He put away the watch in his vest pocket and laid a fatherly hand on the girl's shoulder. His jaw was thrust out, his lips separated, his fine teeth exposed.

"Brace up, child," he said, not unkindly. "I am afraid you have a hard job ahead of you, and Tony and I count on you for the next few hours. It looks as if your roommate was the victim of some insensate, brutish, mad and yet clever criminal. Look around you and you would think he was like a fury let loose, as if rejoicing to lave in the blood of his victim, turning this pretty little house into an abattoir. But that is only the surface. The crime, I believe, was more hideous than that. All this violence and ferocity was premeditated and performed coolly, deliberately, and with calm intention. That is what I believe, at least, and that is what makes it seem so horrible to me. Clever, indeed—yet there are clues here that sooner or later will lead me to the guilty one."

He turned from the girl, who still lingered in the shadows of the doorway, and began emptying his pockets.

"Take these objects, Tony," he said, "and handle them gently—they may point us to the murderer. Sixty-seven per cent of our unsolved murders are committed indoors, but this one I'm going to clear up or—"

Betty turned away as he put into my hands the watch, wrapped in a handkerchief, two envelopes, on each of which the word "hair" had been scribbled, and finally, a white face-cloth on which I observed two horrible scarlet stains.

"I found that face-cloth in the bath-room, too," explained Thatcher Colt. "Handle it with all care—I have a hunch I will use that to good purpose in court some day. Or rather, District Attorney Dougherty, most likely."

He dug deeper into his pockets until satisfied that all his findings were accounted for.

"I'll have more for you later on," promised Thatcher Colt. "Just now I want to—"

He did not finish the sentence, for suddenly Neil McMahon, the Commissioner's chauffeur, towered in the doorway, his moon-like face pale and expressionless as ever. But in his eyes I observed a gleam come and go like Northern lights.

"I have found the grave, Mr. Commissioner," he announced simply.

Without a word, Thatcher Colt followed the chauffeur out of the house, with Betty and me close upon his heels. But at an impatient wave of his hand, Betty remained behind, leaning against the door-post and looking after us through the deepening twilight with frightened eyes, as we plunged into a thicket of trees.

The little light that still lingered in the sky penetrated but dimly into the thinly wooded section that surrounded the house. But Neil McMahon led us confidently through the dimness of the gloaming, spraying in front of him a stream of light from his 300-foot-focus flashlight. I felt a chill of weird apprehension, for the mystery of dusk lay over us in gibbous shadows and gathering dark. Presently we came to a little open space in the trees, and Neil McMahon played his flashlight on what seemed to be a curious and sinister mound. We stood together, the three of us and looked down upon a pile of earth, covered with dried leaves.

Thatcher Colt, who was wearing a topcoat, grey-striped trousers and gloves, knelt and moved his hands among the leaves, feeling his way like a doctor reaching under a garment to touch flesh that is in pain. Swiftly then he pushed aside entire armfuls of leaves, scattering them off into the darkness. They made a gentle, sibilant, murmuring sound as they were dispersed through the air. The earth laid bare to our gaze seemed soft and loose though everything around was frozen and stiff in the grip of winter.

I proposed to run back to the house and fetch the shovel, but Thatcher Colt shook his head disapprovingly.

"I would prefer not to use that spade just now," he said.

Saying this, Thatcher Colt took off his topcoat and gloves. In another moment, the most immaculate dresser in the whole city administration was on the knees of his grey-striped trousers, his fingers spread out, clawing up whole handfuls of the earth. Quickly Neil McMahon and I followed suit, the chauffeur at the head and I at the foot, and Thatcher Colt at one side of the grave, scooping up with palms and fingers the clods of earth. We were working like evil spirits that are said to prey on corpses. So loose lay the earth that we could work with astonishing speed—most of the dirt was thrown up from the grave within fifteen minutes. Suddenly I gave a cry, for my right hand had touched something cold and white and stiff—the bare foot of a human body.

As in a frenzy then we clawed at the earth that lay around that stiff form in the ground. The air was bitter cold, yet the perspiration ran from our foreheads into our eyes. Now that we had found the infernal sepulchre we were seeking, ages seemed to pass before all the earth was taken from it and we could stand up, as we did stand up, panting and gasping, and sick with horror, and look down upon that illuminated trench.

What we had unearthed was the nude form of a girl, its head covered with a pillow case stained with earth and blood, the whole body hideously hacked, and most awfully slain. On one slim finger glistened the diamond of an engagement ring. After the first long, appalling scrutiny, we turned away from that eerie sight, as if by common consent. Neil clutched off the headlight. In the dark we stood there, men who had fought in the front line trenches, men accustomed to death, now momentarily shaken and queachy and sick.

But our hesitancy was only for a moment. Thatcher Colt's own flashlight was suddenly turned on the grave and he knelt on the rim of the shallow pit. Reaching down into the grave, with little, jerky movements, he pulled away the pillow case that shrouded the head. The cruelly battered face looked up at him with its distended sightless eyes.

The Commissioner gently brushed the dirt and hardened blood from the face and scrutinized it intently. Was this the body of Geraldine Foster? The resemblance to the photograph was undeniable.

"The body is nude," cried Thatcher Colt suddenly, "and yet—"

He put his finger on one cruel wound in the right shoulder. Very carefully he disengaged a tenuous piece of thread, imbedded deeply in the flesh.

"There are these almost invisible traces of cloth in several of the axe-cuts," he called back over his shoulder. "Evidently she was fully clothed when she was attacked, and stripped after she was dead. Now, why was that?"

The Commissioner, still on his knees, next became interested in the pillow case. He held the case close to him, playing the rays of the spotlight on it.

"The pillow case is wet," he said aloud, "but not with blood."

For a moment he muttered grimly to himself, and finally said distinctly:

"And this is dry ground. Very dry ground. We have had a prolonged dry spell. What is water doing in this grave? And the smell of pine trees all around? There are no pine trees growing nearby."

He reached in, fumbling about in the earth that lay under the stiff form. He put one hand on the knee and then on the shoulder, and drew it away with a low murmur of wonder.

"The body, too, is wet," he muttered.

Suddenly, he rose, turned to me and said, briskly:

"Tony, I want you to stay here and guard this body. McMahon, come with me."

I watched the two figures retreat through the trees and I stood there, alone, with the wind muttering in the dry branches, and the open grave with its dreadful burden exposed at my feet. It was full dark now and I will confess that I was very cold and lonely.

6
IN THE BAG

The Commissioner had taken the pillow case with him. What could he mean by all those mysterious comments? Why had a pillow case been put over the head of the corpse, leaving all the rest of the tortured body nude? Did this betray a weakness in the killer? I wondered if the explanation was that he could not bear to look upon the mutilated face of his victim.

"Ah, no, Tony," I was later to hear Thatcher Colt assure me. "The pillow case was not weakness—it was strength. It was used deliberately and with diabolical intent."

Through the trees I could see the glimmer of lights in the little house where Geraldine Foster had met her death. Here she lay, in the earth beside me, and I marveled again at the irrevocableness of death. In this dead girl's head, I reflected, there was still a brain and on that brain was left the full impression of the crime and the killer. Yet science knows no way of reading the secrets of a brain that is dead. If it were only possible to extract that brain in a laboratory, subject it to tests and finding the memory records, interpret them, translate them, get full access to them—

Ah, then, I thought, if that were so, the first thing the smart criminals would do would be to cut out the brains of their victims and destroy them.

Such were my ghoulish and fantastic musings, as I stood guard beside the body of the murdered Geraldine Foster.

Suddenly I stopped and listened. Not far away I had heard the rustle of footsteps; and a light gleamed fitfully through the trees.

"Who is there?" I called.

"It is me," said Neil McMahon and a moment later the Commissioner's chauffeur covered me in the glare of his hand-torch. With some astonishment, I observed that he was carrying a small bottle in his right hand.

"What is that for?" I asked.

Without replying, he passed me his flashlight and then dropped into the tenebrous shadows that hovered over the open grave. Lying flat on his stomach, Neil uncorked his bottle and lowered it out of sight. I heard a gurgling sound and then saw him lift the bottle, half-filled with some fluid, and carefully cork it. You can see that bottle, too, exhibited today in the Department's Crime Museum.

As Neil stood up, I was about to repeat my question, when a sudden interruption prevented me. So absorbed had I been in his operations that I had not noticed the approach of others, and now to my astonishment I saw Thatcher Colt approaching with Betty Canfield walking by his side. She threw me a glance of horror and apprehension but she did not speak.

"Just take one look and tell me," said Thatcher Colt, and he put his arm around the girl as they stood together on the brink of the grave. At the sight of the dead body, no loud cry came from Betty, but the low moan of anguish that rose from her lips was as poignant and pitiful as it was conclusive.

"It is Geraldine!" she wailed, and the next moment Thatcher Colt was leading her, almost dragging her away from the grave, with Neil hastening after them. Cruel, but a necessary performance.

For more than half an hour after that, I kept my lonely vigil over the body of Geraldine Foster. Meanwhile I could guess a part, at least, of what was afoot in the house. Neil McMahon, acting on the orders of his chief, had telephoned Headquarters. Already the word had gone forth through the various channels of the gruesome find Colt had turned up. To the Bureau of Criminal Information the news had been flashed, and to all others concerned. Even now detectives were on their way to us from the Borough Homicide Squad, with their police photographers and stenographers; the Medical Examiner or one of his assistants had been summoned and with him would certainly appear the Inspector commanding the Detective Division in the locality where the body lay, and probably the Captain of the Precinct, as well. And some one from the District Attorney's office was headed for us, too, with a detective assigned to aid him. All this machinery of the law was set in motion by Thatcher Colt's telephone call to Assistant Chief Inspector (now Commissioner) Edward P. Mulrooney. Meanwhile, as he awaited the coming battalions, I knew that Thatcher Colt returned to his solitary quest, carefully noting all the existing conditions, the signs of the struggle, the weapon—the hunter was already started on a private trail which was eventually to lead him into incredible discoveries.

Though it was only half an hour, it seemed to me that I had stood guard for hours before I saw, far down through the trees, the flashing of lights and heard the rumble of many voices. Thatcher Colt strode forward, leading a procession of officials, patrolmen, plainclothes men and others from the Department. In a few moments, a dozen pocket electric lamps were blazing like toy comets around the grave. The place was transformed from a desolate spot to something like a camp, full of important activities. Thatcher Colt, in personal command, had ordered the

entire plateau of undeveloped land roped off, so that
possible footprints and other traces—later found to be
non-existent—might be safeguarded against trampling
feet. In the group that stood around the Police Commissioner was David Gallop, from the District Attorney's
office, Inspector Crester, from the Detective Division,
Doctor Multooler, an Assistant Medical Examiner, a group
of plainclothes men, and a number of patrolmen. A photographer from the Department was setting up his camera
and focusing, and soon blast after blast of lighted smoke
flashed up in acrid plumes through the trees as the flashlight pictures were taken from various angles of the body.
The photographer then left us, to take pictures of the
wreckage within the house.

Under Colt's orders, some of the detectives began a me-
ticulous search of the surrounding land, not waiting until
dawn but prowling with flashlights in organized sections.
Still others were delegated to repeat the Commissioner's
search of the house. Meanwhile, two patrolmen were hoist-
ing the body from the grave. They carried it back to the
house and heaved it up on a white enameled table in the
kitchen. There at the request of Thatcher Colt, the Assistant Medical Examiner agreed to make a preliminary
examination.

"How long do you think she has been dead?" asked
Thatcher Colt, after we had waited in silence for perhaps
five minutes.

Doctor Multooler looked around over his shoulder and
replied:

"I can only guess until I make an autopsy. But I would
say not more than thirty-six hours."

Thatcher Colt's face expressed the deepest amazement.

"Thirty-six hours!" he repeated. "That seems impossible!"

The doctor smiled with an air of superior knowledge.

"Impossible, Mr. Commissioner? The state of the body tells me it has not been dead more than forty-eight hours, at the utmost."

Thatcher Colt made no reply, but his somber eyes, staring into space, seemed to be contemplating some infernal mystery that puzzled and horrified him.

He remained there, while a detective, at his orders, scraped the refuse from under the dead girl's fingernails and deposited it in separate envelopes, each marked to identify the finger and hand from which it had been taken. This procedure, a piece of modern police technique, has helped in the solution of many baffling crimes, but in no case did it play a more erratic part than in the curious mystery in which we were now entangled. Then Sergeant Wickes, from the Statistical and Criminal Identification Bureau, inked the dead girl's finger tips and took the black impression of her whorls and loops.

Meanwhile, Neil McMahon had been filling in the blank spaces on a tag known in the Department as U. F. No. 95, which is placed on the wrist or great toe of all dead bodies in homicide cases.

Finally, the body was carried out to a patrol wagon, waiting to carry it downtown, and Doctor Multooler proposed at once to follow it.

"When can I have your final report?" asked Thatcher Colt, as the doctor was departing.

"Some time before morning. Shall I send it to you and not to the District Attorney?"

"Please send it to my office at Headquarters. I shall be waiting for it."

The Assistant Medical Examiner looked a little bewildered, but bowed and departed.

We heard the two cars snorting and driving off down the narrow descent of Peddler's Road, while Thatcher Colt and I stood in the kitchen and waited for reports. Already

the hunt was organized, with that skillful military precision which Thatcher Colt had brought into the Department. Just as the woods were being scoured, so every detail of the house was also being gone over. Some of the
men were making notes of the surroundings, with special
regard to the distance and relative position of house and
grave, trees and road. Maps were actually being drawn of
these things, some day to be enlarged and shown to a jury,
maps of the position of the house, the layout of the rooms,
even the position of the furniture—encyclopedic details of
the crime and its locale were being assembled.

One of the first results of this systematic search was
the finding of two large bottles, several hundred feet distant from the grave. They were brought in by Detective
Schwaab, and Thatcher Colt received them with great interest.

"Remember," he said, "that Geraldine Foster—or at
least a girl resembling her—was seen leaving the house in
Washington Square, in company with another woman—
and both carried large bottles, just like this, and also just
like another in the back room of Maskell's suite of offices.
We should give more thought to those bottles, later, Tony."

He paused and smiled at me.

"For your peace of mind," he disclosed, "I have sent
Betty Canfield down to Headquarters to wait for us. There
are some questions she will have to answer tonight. I am
sorry to say that I had to procure her attendance for the
autopsy, so that she can identify the body, and I have also
telephoned for the poor parents of the dead girl for the
same purpose. I shall also have to question them. Meanwhile, I think I hear the stentorian boom of a familiar
voice."

The next moment there came through the doorway, a
huge man with curly red hair, large, bold, blue eyes and

prognathous jaw. The newcomer shook hands grimly with the Police Commissioner. He was that vital and magnetic Merle Dougherty who was such a firebrand while he was District Attorney. "Hot-spur" was Thatcher Colt's adjective for him. The two men disagreed on almost every known subject, with the exception of their liking for certain German beers and their admiration for each other.

Dougherty was known to have high political ambitions, and it was freely predicted that he would be Governor of New York before he received extreme unction. He had a high respect for a legally-trained mind, no patience with abstractions of any kind, and feared indecision as some men fear poverty. I soon learned that Dougherty had kept himself informed about the police search for Geraldine Foster and was fairly familiar with many details of the case.

"Well, Colt," he said, "your hunch was right. It was murder—and a pretty messy one. I have decided to take personal charge of the affair, and you mark my words, I shall bring the murderer to the electric chair so quickly that it will be a lesson to the whole country."

Thatcher Colt emptied his pipe and proceeded to refill it as he replied:

"I shall certainly be glad to have your cooperation, Dougherty."

"What do you mean by that?" blurted the District Attorney.

"I thought I might take a hand in solving this business myself," drawled Thatcher Colt.

"Conflict of authority?" barked Dougherty.

"Not at all, old fellow. As the ranking head of the Force, I am merely doing my constitutional duty. Never forget that it is written in the book, the commanding officer shall be held responsible for the completeness of the investigation."

"You know it isn't done, though," protested the District Attorney. "However, I shall be glad to have your help. Now, what's what?"

"Isn't Hogan with you?" asked Colt.

"Sure!"—and a little man with a bald, ovoid head, stepped quickly through the door. He was Dougherty's favorite detective, a County Detective with more than ordinary wits, assigned to the District Attorney's office. In his hands I noticed that he held a white package, tied with red ribbon.

"Hogan might as well listen, too," explained Colt, and then, in a brisk and magnificently compressed statement, he gave the District Attorney a complete conspectus of the crime, from the first appearance of Betty Canfield at Headquarters down to the finding of the corpse.

"Some lover of hers did it," said Dougherty promptly. "He probably got the girl in trouble, then lured her up here and killed her. There's too much of this sort of thing going on—too many crimes of passion."

"Perhaps," murmured Thatcher Colt.

"Plain as the nose on your face," declared Dougherty. "All we have to do is to find who owns this house and have a talk with some of her boy friends."

Thatcher Colt lit his pipe.

"Yes," he said. "And by the way, Hogan, I know you think you have a clue in that package you have there. Is that a Christmas present you have found?"

"Yes, it is—it's a silk muffler," said Hogan. "I found it under the sofa. I would like to hang on to it for a while, if you don't mind."

"Not at all—I've already had a look at it," answered Colt agreeably. "Also, I have telephoned downtown and found that this house is owned by a Mrs. Haberhorn, who rents it out. It will be as you say, simple to find out the name of her tenant—if the tenant gave her his real name.

And, by the way, I am temporarily removing some evidence from the scene."

He lifted the pillow case and flung it over his shoulder.

"What's inside the bag?" asked Dougherty promptly.

"Seven dead pigeons," answered Thatcher Colt. "About midnight join me at Headquarters, will you, Dougherty, and we will go over what we have. Mind?"

"Okay," said Dougherty, and added after a moment's thoughtful pause, "if I haven't arrested the murderer before then."

"You won't!" chuckled the Commissioner, and with a nod to me, he led the way down to the street.

7

THE MAN WHO JUSTIFIED MURDER

Having eluded the ambush of a squad of newspaper reporters, waiting to obtain Thatcher Colt's personal version of
the Peddler's Road affair, we hurried on toward the Commissioner's office. As we entered the octagonal reception
room, with its old-fashioned wood-work and its transoms
of stained glass, a curious sight met our eyes.

Most of the people concerned in the mystery of Geraldine Foster were gathered before us, their haggard eyes
staring up into our faces. For the moment, I was startled at the sight of such an organized and appropriate
convocation. Then I realized that by the telephoned orders of Thatcher Colt all these people had been quickly
brought to Headquarters. Seeing the Commissioner, the
father and mother of the murdered girl stood up with pa-
thetic promptness. They guessed the truth without having
been told. Thatcher Colt spoke to them briefly and in low
tones, while my glance leaped around the room. Among
the others gathered in the waiting room were two young
men whom I judged to be Bruce Foster and Harry Armstrong. Neither resembled Geraldine, so I could not tell
which was the brother and which the lover. Aloof from
these others and looking pale and worn sat Betty Canfield.

With another reassuring word to the parents, Thatcher
Colt hastened on into his private office and I followed

him. On the desk he laid the pillow case with the dead pigeons.

Then he dashed on into a small retiring room—a partition affair built for his personal use—and almost instantly I heard the sound of rushing water. Mr. Colt was taking a shower. In an amazingly short time, he came out again, completely re-dressed, as immaculate and fashionable as if the hour were morning and he were just reporting for work.

Meanwhile, I had been busy. I laid out on the desk the various objects I had carried—among them the envelopes of hair, the face cloth with the crimson stains, the watch, and the axe, which I had wrapped in a newspaper.

For the next few minutes I was busy on the telephone, calling various officers for the Commissioner. Presently the Deputy Chief Inspector arrived, followed by Doctor Clesleek, one of the most scholarly chemists attached to the office of the Medical Examiner.

Without parley, Thatcher Colt issued a series of crisp, precise orders. He wanted the owner of the house on Peddler's Road found at once and brought downtown. A detective must also be sent to Wisner's, a chemist's shop on Madison Avenue, to find out what was contained in three large bottles sent upon the urgent request of Doctor Maskell on Christmas Eve.

"Funny thing," added Thatcher Colt. "Damned funny thing. You might add that those bottles smelt like the bark of pine trees."

Without pausing for comment, he then gave instructions for examining the refuse pared from under the nails of the corpse and the hairs contained in two envelopes. Then he called Doctor Clesleek aside and in a low voice communicated certain other instructions, not a word of which I could distinguish. Also something passed from the hand of the detective to the hand of the chemist. I caught a glimpse of that—it was the wash-cloth found in the murder house.

"What you ask is almost impossible," said Doctor Clesleek. "But I will do my best."

Colt next made a most extraordinary request of Doctor Clesleek.

"In the pillow case on my desk are some dead pigeons, Doctor," he said. "Can you examine dead pigeons and make a guess as to how long they have been dead?"

"An autopsy on pigeons?"

"Mind?"

"No," sighed Doctor Clesleek, "I'll do my best as always."

Following the officers, Clesleek, his arms full of dead birds, left the room.

"Ah, Tony," Colt cried, "I wonder if those blundering fellows up on Peddler's Road have found Geraldine's clothes yet. I assigned three of them just for that job. Now let me see. The Deputy Chief Inspector took the envelope with the parings from her nails. They will show us something, too, I hope."

His eyes were gleaming with the zest of the hunter, as he sat at his desk and lit his pipe.

"Ask that poor old couple to come in, Tony."

Mr. and Mrs. Foster trudged into the office and sat in chairs before the Commissioner's desk. They were making a great effort to hold on to their composure. Very gently Thatcher Colt gave them a part of the story. Then he began urging upon them the importance of their remaining calm in the face of the tragedy and giving what help they could to the Department.

"Mr. Colt," rumbled old Edmund L. Foster, raising his red hands over his head, "whatever happens, my daughter was a good girl, and don't forget that!"

His voice was deep and vibrating with great feeling. His wife did not look at him. With her two hands laid against her breasts, she stared fixedly through her glasses. But there were no tears on the strained face of the mother.

"I am sure that Geraldine was a good girl," returned Thatcher Colt earnestly. "But, Mr. Foster, you remember the key that we found in her pocket. Are you sure that you know nothing of that key?"

"Nothing," avouched Mr. Foster in his impassioned bass.

Thatcher Colt then explained that the key fitted the house on Peddler's Road. He questioned the father about the friends and acquaintances of his daughter. Mr. Foster liked them all. He thought Betty Canfield was a sweet little girl, Harry Armstrong was a smart young fellow and, as for Doctor Maskell, he had treated Geraldine as fine as any girl could want. The father had a good word even for Checkles, the chauffeur, for whom Geraldine had manifested a pitying kindness.

"Was Geraldine in any financial distress?"

"Bosh and bunk!" thundered the father. "I am not a poor man. I have one hundred thousand dollars to my name and half of it would have gone to my girl when I died. She must have been crazy when she wrote that note you found. Why, she knew I was going to give her ten thousand as a wedding present. And she knew she could come to her old father for anything. But now she's gone and she will never enjoy a penny of all that money."

After a moment of silence, Thatcher Colt inquired:

"Who will inherit her share?"

"All of it goes to my boy Bruce, now. Every cent," declared Foster with a wave of his immense red hands.

"Was Bruce your first child, Mrs. Foster?" asked Thatcher Colt.

The old woman clapped her hands quickly together, as does one who is taken by surprise, and her crimpled cheeks quivered with sudden inexplicable emotion.

"Bruce is not my first child," she said hastily, rolling her unhappy eyes.

Just then a knock sounded on the door and Captain Henry announced that the Medical Examiner had sent for the parents of the dead girl. The Commissioner shook hands with them, promising to see them the next day, and sent them forth on one of the saddest errands that can come to mortal kind.

"Well, Tony, if you are looking for motives for the murder, you have two now."

"Two, Chief? I don't get you."

"Yes. There is the possibility of the Virginius motive."

"Virginius?"

"Yes—the father who places such store on chastity that he would kill a violated daughter. Rare in these days—but you have heard Edmund L. Foster speak twice for himself."

"I hadn't thought of that—it doesn't sound reasonable—and yet—"

"Ah, yes, Tony! There is always that 'and yet!'"

"But the other motive?"

"Bruce Foster might have killed the girl to get her share of the inheritance. He would not be the first brother to do such a thing."

"That is a horrible thought—a brother to kill a sister for money?"

Instead of replying, my chief told me to bring Bruce Foster in to the office.

The young man who stalked in so boldly was tall and thin but he looked strong. He had sandy hair, ruddy complexion and challenging blue eyes. In his very walk there was an air of truculence as if he were determined to prove to the world that he was not afraid of it. As the door swung shut behind him, he thrust forward his head, exposing his teeth and said to Thatcher Colt:

"This is a hell of a way to treat white people. You send my father and mother to the Morgue to look at the body of Gerry, before they cut her up with their damned knives, but you won't let me go along with them to stand by and catch them when they fall. Talk about Prussianism!"

"Sit down," said Thatcher Colt crisply.

Bruce Foster flung himself into the chair and glared defiance at the Commissioner.

"Your sister has been murdered," said Thatcher Colt, "and you are needed right here. I know it is hard on your parents. But the police need you right now."

"What for?"

"I want you to tell me what you know."

"What *I* know? I don't know anything."

Thatcher Colt shook his head.

"We'll never get anywhere that way," he remonstrated.

"Why? Do you accuse me of holding anything back?"

"You thought your sister was having an affair. You didn't want your father to know. So you started to settle the matter for yourself. Whom did you think she had an affair with?"

The ruddy cheeks of the young man turned pale.

"Who told you that?" he demanded.

"I guessed it," said Thatcher Colt truthfully. "Whom did you suspect, Bruce?"

The boy shrugged his shoulders.

"You guessed wrong," he answered stubbornly.

"Where did you go when you wouldn't tell your father and mother where you would search for your sister?" insisted Thatcher Colt.

The boy turned his eyes away and would not answer. After watching him for a moment in silence, Thatcher

Colt suddenly rose and passed behind the screen. When he emerged, he fixed Bruce Foster with a glance.

"Bruce, I had one report on you from Betty Canfield. She used to like you. But she broke her engagement with you. She said you used to be a fine fellow, but you turned into a hellion, a good-for-nothing fellow, all at once. Hitting the booze pretty hard. Almost lost your job as an accountant out at Millbrink. Now don't sit there like a churl and refuse to talk to me. Didn't you take to drinking because you believed your sister was leading an immoral life?"

As Bruce looked up at the Commissioner, his face was like a minnesinger in a medieval painting.

"What has that to do with the murder?" he asked.

But Thatcher Colt was relentless.

"Does that refresh your memory?" he asked, and tossed the key on the glass top of the desk, where it fell with a ringing sound.

At the sight of the key, with the string of blue ribbon, the young man's face remained impassive.

Thatcher Colt bent over him, his two hands seizing the shoulders firmly.

"Whose key is that? To whose door?" he demanded.

Bruce Foster shut his eyes to avoid the commanding stare of Thatcher Colt's somber eyes. He clasped his hands together and moved his feet back and forth restlessly.

"I never saw it before," he declared.

"All right," said Thatcher Colt, pushing the key aside. "Tell me where you went to look for your sister."

"I was just a fool," said Bruce bitterly. "I've got a bad temper and I know it. But I will tell you all about it. I knew that things hadn't been going well between Gerry and the fellow she was going to marry. The wedding was almost here and the nearer it came the more miserable she seemed. But she wouldn't tell me what the trouble was, nor pop, nor mom. She would make it up with Harry and everything would be all right and then the next time we saw her she was sad and blue. On Christmas Eve I was in New York and I called her up. I was going to take her home with me for Christmas. But she was crying over the phone and said she didn't care what happened to her. I said I would come right up but she told me not to."

"What time was that?" asked Colt casually.

"A little after two o'clock in the afternoon."

"What did you do then?"

"I just walked around the town, looking in the shop windows, and I took in a movie, trying to cheer myself up."

"Did you buy anything?"

"No, sir."

"And when you learned that your sister was really missing, where did you go to look for her? This is the third time I've asked you that question!"

"I went to Harry Armstrong's apartment. That was the day pop and mom came into New York and talked with you. I suspected Harry. I didn't know what might have happened to Gerry. I was ready to have it out with him. But I couldn't locate him. And since I've talked with pop and mom, I know I was a big fool. There wasn't anything wrong between Gerry and Harry. I'm ashamed ever to have thought such a thing. How did you know I did?"

Thatcher Colt replied with a question:

"Whom else did you question about it?"

A look of surprise flushed Bruce's face as he exclaimed: "Betty!"

Before Thatcher Colt could proceed, a rap came at the door and Captain Henry came in, carrying a small envelope which he laid very carefully on the desk.

"From Doctor Multooler," he said. "You asked for them, he says. From the dead girl's mouth."

Bruce Foster averted his gaze as Thatcher Colt gingerly opened the envelope. He peered inside, and I was close enough also to see that the envelope contained some minute particles of some dried, red, flaky substance.

"Take these to Clesleek," ordered the Commissioner. "Tell him I want the brand established at the earliest possible moment."

Captain Henry saluted and retired, carrying the envelope far out from him at the tips of his pudgy fingers. While I was wondering at this strange incident, Thatcher Colt turned back to Bruce Foster.

"Maybe you are not telling me everything?" he asked, with a melancholy glance. "Anyway, you will, sooner or later. Now, Bruce, I want you to get your mother and father and take them home. Give them something to make them sleep tonight. But I want you back here tomorrow morning."

Bruce promised and left the room, considerably chastened. Thatcher Colt's eyes, now turned to mine, held a cryptic expression.

"Tony," he said, shaking his head, as if by that motion to throw from his soul the shadow of an evil influence, "let's forget that boy just now. I am sometimes a telepathist. I now hereby read your mind and know that you wish I would talk to Betty Canfield next and get through with her so that the young lady can go home."

"Right," I exclaimed, and bounded for the door. My heart smote me at the sight of the woe-begone little figure that I saw slumped in the chair. But the brisk way she stood up, and the sad smile of friendship she gave me, quickened my admiration.

Thatcher Colt received her with a pleasant wave of his hand.

"Betty," he began, "I am coming right to the point with you. You have not been frank with me from the start, child, but now you must realize that you have to be. Why did you and Geraldine quarrel the day before she disappeared?"

Her shocked expression betrayed how greatly taken by surprise she was. But Thatcher Colt gave her no time.

"No evasions. What was it about?"

"Mr. Colt, I don't want to tell you."

"This is murder!"

"Even so, I can't tell you."

"Then let me tell you," said Thatcher Colt. "One of your neighbors overheard you and told one of my men. It was about Bruce Foster and his suspicions of his sister's morals, was it not?"

Betty would not speak. Even though she was disobeying my chief, I had to admire her loyalty to her dead friend, and so, I think, did Thatcher Colt.

"Bruce thought Geraldine had an affair with Harry Armstrong—and that he had thrown her over and refused to marry her. He first came to you about it. You told Geraldine—and that started the quarrel."

Thankfully Betty Canfield looked up at the Commissioner.

"Now, Betty, can you tell me Geraldine was innocent?"

"Absolutely."

"But the engagement was broken?"

"Yes—they kept meeting, trying to patch up whatever it was they quarreled about."

"Do you know what it was?"

"No."

"All right. We'll pass all that. Have you a lease on your apartment on Morningside Heights?"

"Yes."

"How long does it run?"

"Until next May."

"Then you intend to sublet it?"

"Yes, I have been trying for the last two months."

"Who exhibits the apartment when you are at work?"

"The janitor, or one of the elevator boys."

Dropping this, Thatcher Colt asked:

"When was the last time Harry Armstrong telephoned your apartment?"

"Harry telephoned twice about three o'clock on Saturday morning," she answered.

"You mean the early morning hours of Christmas Eve?"

"Yes."

"But how is that possible? Where did he telephone from? He was supposed to be on the night train to Boston."

"That's odd. You know I hadn't thought of that before, Mr. Colt."

Thatcher Colt lit his pipe, which had gone out. Dismissing the former line of questions, he resumed:

"Now tell me the real reason why you meet Doctor Maskell with the frappé glance and the glacé manner? You fibbed to me the last time you were down here. You said you didn't like him, but didn't know why. But I doubted that yarn, Betty. What makes you dislike the doctor?"

She stood up and held out her hand.

"If I tell you, will you let me go home?"

"Promise!"

"Because Doctor Maskell often told Geraldine that he believed murder justified under certain circumstances. By the way she repeated it, I think he meant it, and since I heard that I could never bear the sight of him."

"Indeed!" said Thatcher Colt, softly.

8
A STRANGE SECRET

With one backward glance at me, Betty left the office.
Thatcher Colt remained moodily at his desk, toying with
the blue ribbon of the key.

"Our motives accumulate, Tony," he remarked.

"Are there any that I hadn't noticed?"

"Plenty of them. Now let's have a look at Harry Armstrong."

The fiancé of the murdered Geraldine was a young man
of medium height, with greenish-blue eyes, curly brown
hair, and a slightly supercilious air. It was quite evident
that he resented being called to Police Headquarters. But
in spite of the rather top-lofty attitude that Armstrong as-
sumed, it was easy to see and appraise the tragic, wounded
expression that glowed in his handsome eyes.

As always, Thatcher Colt began by trying to win his
confidence. In a murder mystery such as this, the Commissioner explained, the police placed their chief reliance
on the frankness of the friends of the slain person. He
hoped he might count on Mr. Armstrong to answer all
questions freely.

"You may," said the young man, laconically but with
sharp emphasis.

"Your parents live in Boston?"

"My mother lives there."

"Father dead?"

"Yes."

"All right," he said. "Now, tell me about yourself."

Armstrong was a bond salesman with Fisher and Clark, a large securities firm in the Wall Street district. He had first met Geraldine Foster two years before at a dance. Their friendship ripened until they finally became engaged. They had made their plans to be married on the day after New Year's.

"Had you made any preparations for your new living quarters?" asked Thatcher Colt.

"Of course. Ever since I have been in New York, I have lived in two old-fashioned rooms in a house on East Sixty-ninth Street. Geraldine and I had decided to go right on living there."

Thatcher Colt fixed his somber dark eyes directly on the young man.

"Were there intimate, pre-marital arrangements between you and Geraldine Foster?" he asked.

"Bruce Foster has been talking to you!" cried Armstrong angrily.

With great deliberation, Thatcher Colt emptied his pipe, and slowly re-filled it before speaking again.

"You know, Armstrong," he said, "I am glad to find such old-fashioned, sensitiveness about such matters. Lots of people today consider trial marriage and things like that wholly respectable. But apparently that isn't true of Bruce Foster, old Mr. Foster, or yourself."

"Or Geraldine!" exclaimed Armstrong simply and vigorously.

"Suppose she *had* been intimate with another man?" said Thatcher Colt suddenly. A deep pallor crossed the young face, and beads of milky perspiration stood on his brow.

"I won't discuss that," he said huskily.

"Good!" agreed Thatcher Colt. "Now I want to ask you about your own movements recently. On Friday night, December 23, you took the midnight train out of Grand Central Station. Is that correct?"

"It is."

"Yet I understand that you telephoned Geraldine a few hours later. Is that correct?"

"Yes, that's correct, too."

"Where did you telephone from, Armstrong?"

"From Hartford."

"You left the train at Hartford?"

"Yes."

"Why?"

"I was worried."

Thatcher Colt threw up his hands.

"Armstrong," he remonstrated, "are you going to make me drag every fact out of you? Tell me what happened, for the love of God, and stop being so hostile."

Armstrong shrugged his shoulders, folded his arms and sat up a little straighter.

"Well, Geraldine and I had had several little misunderstandings," he admitted. "I finally decided I was all wrong and so I got off the train, called up and suggested that we go off and elope and show up Christmas morning at my mother's house as man and wife."

"And she refused? Why?"

"Because she was still angry. I hung up. Then I got lonesome and morbid. I had a few drinks and it made me feel very angry. I had to prove that Geraldine loved me. So I called her apartment again and we had the whole argument all over again."

"And she still refused you?"

"Yes," said Harry Armstrong bitterly, "she did. If she hadn't, she might be alive today."

"Quite correct," agreed Thatcher Colt. "Now what did you do after the telephone call?"

"I found a speak-easy," confessed the young man, "and I drank myself into insensibility."

"Well, where were you when you regained your senses?"

"In New York City, in Grand Central Station."

"When was that?"

"Christmas Eve, around six o'clock."

"What had you been doing meanwhile?"

"I don't know."

Thatcher Colt sat up straighter and looked sharply at the young man.

"Do you mean to tell me," he said, "that you cannot account for your movements from the time you had the telephone call with Geraldine, and six o'clock Christmas Eve?"

"That is correct, Mr. Colt."

"Do you realize," said the Commissioner, "that the girl vanished within that time?"

"I certainly do."

Harry Armstrong then lit a cigarette, and added:

"But can you think of any sensible reason why I should kill the girl I loved?"

The Commissioner's face was contracted into thoughtful ridges for a moment.

"Well, Armstrong," he said, "I am sorry you cannot give a clearer account of your movements. It makes it difficult for you and for us, too. What was the cause of your disagreement with Geraldine?"

"I can't answer that."

"But you will have to, before you get through."

"Nevertheless, I refuse. I will only tell you this. Bruce Foster is not Geraldine's brother. I quarreled with Geraldine because I was a snob, and I regret it. Bruce is an adopted child."

Thatcher Colt looked at the young man inscrutably.

"You are not telling me the whole truth!"

"No—and I don't intend to."

"Then I am sorry—I shall have to turn you over to some of our men for a long night of questioning."

"The third degree?" asked Harry Armstrong, in a low voice.

"Some people call it that."

"I'm not afraid of being beaten up."

"Good," said Thatcher Colt, pressing the buzzer, and then talking into the silent, inter-office phone. Soon Captain Henry led Harry Armstrong away. As soon as we were left alone, Thatcher Colt was on the telephone calling the Chief of Police of Wingsboro, Maryland. I waited while he held a long conversation, during which I caught the name of Bruce Foster. The Commissioner, who is always like lightning on the telephone, lingered during this conversation, and when he finally turned to me, it was evident that he expected to learn something of importance. Presently, there was a lull and he turned to me.

"We are in luck," he said. "The Chief of Police has a brother who knew the Foster family well when they lived in that town. He is getting the brother to the telephone. Get on the extension phone and listen in."

This is what I heard:

"Helloa, Mr. Colt . . . I've found out all you want to know about the Foster family adopting that child. . . . They named him Bruce. . . . Yeah, that's right. . . . Well, his own mother died when he was born. His father was hung down here—I saw him hung—what's that? Oh, what for? For an axe murder down here— One of the worst murders in the whole history of this here now state. . . . Yeah! Another thing, people down here always said old Mr. Foster was the boy's real father. . . . Anything else. . . ."

"Thanks, nothing else," said Thatcher Colt, brushing the back of his hand across his forehead as he hung up the receiver. His somber eyes were very grave as he turned and groped for his pipe.

I was about to ask Thatcher Colt several questions that bedeviled my mind almost beyond endurance when we were again interrupted by the entrance of Captain Henry. The elderly officer seemed rather excited.

"The woman who owns the house on Peddler's Road is found and here," he announced, and at a quick nod from the Commissioner, he turned and hastened to admit her.

Mrs. Haberhorn was a shabbily dressed old woman, with a voice like a tugboat captain's, and a breath like a still. But she did her best in public to be a perfect lady. Her hair, probably grey, had recently been dyed a rich brown, and her blue eyes glittered suspiciously.

Blinking up at the Commissioner, she said:

"You can't hold me for anything. You don't expect I can ask for the marriage license of everybody I do business with, do you? All I want is my money, and if you don't think I am an honest person, ask any of the policemen on our beat. They'll tell you."

After we had calmed her down, we learned that Mrs. Haberhorn kept a rooming house on West One Hundred and Twenty-Second Street. Apparently she was a miserly person, who dressed poorly to hide her affluence. She also owned the plot of ground on Peddler's Road, which she had held for twelve years as an investment. Two years ago she had rented the ground to a tenant who put up the portable house in which Geraldine Foster had been slain.

"What was the name of the tenant of your property, Mrs. Haberhorn?" asked Thatcher Colt.

"He said he was a Mr. Bigsbee. But why don't you ask him yourself? He's right outside your office this very minute."

"Here?" cried Thatcher Colt, springing to his feet. "Show him to me!"

We followed Mrs. Haberhorn to the door and through it she pointed to a man, smiling blandly at us from his chair in the outer room.

He was the missing Doctor Humphrey Maskell.

9

THE OWNER OF THE MURDER HOUSE

In spite of the grimly controlled expression on the face of my chief, I knew instinctively that Thatcher Colt was taken by surprise, almost as much as I. Not for a moment had I suspected that the "laughing physician of Washington Square" had returned to New York.

Apparently Doctor Maskell did not realize the seriousness of the identification just made of him by his landlady.

"Good evening, Mrs. Haberhorn," he said urbanely. "You seemed as if you did not want to recognize me when you passed me going in just now."

"I shall want to talk with you in just a minute, Doctor," said Thatcher Colt.

"I felt sure of it," replied Maskell, with a wide and complaisant smile.

Without answering, the Police Commissioner backed into his office, and Mrs. Haberhorn followed him.

"How long did you say that man had rented your place, Mrs. Haberhorn?"

"About two years."

"What does he use the house for?"

"What should he use it for?" countered the landlady indignantly. "What's he done wrong up there? Not arson, for the love of God?"

"No—not arson, just a little murder. Pretty girl chopped up with an axe. You don't want to get mixed up in that, do you?"

Mrs. Haberhorn got very red in the face, then as suddenly paled; she threw out her hands and fell backward in a stupor on the floor. Captain Henry and I had to carry Mrs. Haberhorn out, a proceeding which Doctor Maskell watched with lofty curiosity. Leaving Mrs. Haberhorn with the Captain, and instructing him to restore her, but to keep her in the building until further orders, I hurried back to the office. There I found that the immediate questioning of Doctor Maskell was, for the moment, delayed. Thatcher Colt was shaking hands with Merle Dougherty, whose face was now almost as red as his curls, and who seemed bursting with some concealed excitement. Behind the District Attorney stood the bald-headed Hogan, smiling secretively, but his eyes seemed to say that he was only biding his time.

"I've gone over pretty nearly everything up at the house," announced Dougherty, rubbing his hands as if he were congratulating himself. "And Colt, old fellow, I think I can tell you that I think our work is nearly done."

"Really?" Colt looked startled.

"Yes," boomed the District Attorney, with a radiant smile at Hogan. "I think, my dear Colt, that we have come pretty close to the solution. All we have to do now is to find the guilty man and put the handcuffs on him."

"Ah! Is that all?" sighed Thatcher Colt, with a faint smile, as he dropped back into his chair.

"You remember the package wrapped in red ribbon and white paper?"

"The muffler that was so obviously a Christmas present?"

"Yes, sir. Well I examined that parcel and found that it came from Dittery and Flux, the Fifth Avenue haberdashers. At once I shot Hogan out on that job, while I sought other clues on the scene of the crime. Hogan traced the manager of the store, had the store opened up, traced the sales slips and found the name of the purchaser of that identical silk muffler! Now, Mr. Colt, is that quick work, or isn't it?"

Dougherty's eyes were glittering with triumph, and he took a few steps back and forth, making also a slight inclination of his head, as if bowing in acknowledgment of plaudits to his own superior detective powers.

"And the name was Humphrey Maskell," supplemented Thatcher Colt softly.

Dougherty stopped instantly in his walk and glared sidewise at the Police Commissioner.

"Who told *you* that?" he demanded.

"There was a card attached to the package, signed by Doctor Maskell, and wishing one of his patients a very Merry Christmas. If you had only mentioned it—"

Taking the card from his vest pocket, the Commissioner tossed it carelessly on the table.

"Hell and hot water!" shouted Dougherty. "Is this what you call cooperation? Why didn't you tell us about that card?"

"Because I first wanted to find out what it meant," answered Colt, with a sharp glance at his old friend.

"It means that the doctor was on the scene—and it probably means he is as guilty as red hell!"

Thatcher Colt lifted a gently deprecating hand. "Perhaps he is. At least there is much more evidence besides your muffler to point that way."

"For instance?" snapped Dougherty.

The door opened to admit an attendant, who spread out on a side table the damp prints of the official photographs, taken a few hours before at the grave and in the house. Thatcher Colt stood beside Dougherty, his hand on the shoulder of his impetuous friend, as they studied together those grisly scenes.

"Bear with me, Dougherty," pleaded Thatcher Colt. "I am beginning to believe this is a crime far more awful than we have for one instant supposed. We must not be in a hurry this time."

"Tell me what you have found out," proposed Dougherty, his voice slightly less acescent, as he sat down and lit a fresh cigar.

"I can't tell you everything just yet," stipulated Colt, and then with his singular genius for condensation, he gave the District Attorney, including with his glances also the sullen Hogan, a résumé of what had happened since our return to Headquarters. When the summary of Bruce Foster's interview was told to Dougherty, and especially the coincidence of his father's axe murder in the mountains of Maryland, the District Attorney put his head on the side and half closed one eye. Then he learned about Harry Armstrong, the quarrel with Geraldine, and the fact that the murdered girl's fiancé could not account for his movements during the mysterious hours of Christmas Eve. For a moment, the District Attorney looked interested, but then his face grew skeptical.

"The muffler is the real clue," he said. "If we could only find Maskell."

"Besides," put in Hogan, with withering sarcasm, "the boy's ignorance of where he was on Christmas Eve has nothing to do with this case. The girl has been dead only 48 hours at the longest. You heard the Medical Examiner say that. What the District Attorney's office wants to know is where was the Armstrong guy during the last 48 hours?"

With his somber brown eyes, Colt cast upon Hogan a melancholy glance. He was Hogan's chief, but since the detective had been assigned to the District Attorney's office, Hogan felt himself almost ready to be admitted to the bar. The Commissioner smiled forgivingly.

"The Police Commissioner's office, however, will want to know what Geraldine Foster did, where she went, and with whom, from the moment she left Washington Square on the afternoon of December 24 until she died," he stated crisply.

"Maskell can tell you all that. Why don't you ask Maskell? Why don't you find him? Why don't you at least look for him!" cried Dougherty, with his beefy hands tearing at his curls.

Thatcher Colt leaned forward and stared earnestly at his impulsive friend.

"I know we can build a case against Maskell," he conceded—"most likely we shall have to. But if you act hastily, you may soon wish you had waited. Now, Dougherty, if you go after the doctor, you will get your best evidence from me, anyhow. But, on the other hand—"

Thatcher Colt got up from his desk, came around and put his hand on the District Attorney's shoulder. "Stand by and let me finish the rest of the job. If Maskell is guilty, let's cinch the case."

"How long do you want?"

"Twenty-four hours."

"If Maskell were under surveillance, I wouldn't mind delaying but—"

"All right, Dougherty. Would you like to talk to him?"

"When?"

"Now."

"Where?"

"Here. Tony, bring in Doctor Humphrey Maskell."

Into Thatcher Colt's office I led the "laughing physician of Washington Square," while Dougherty stared in dumb amazement.

To his full height stood Humphrey Maskell; his hat was held against his heart, his chin was uplifted so that he reminded me of a politician on the rear platform of a Pullman about to make a speech.

"Sit down, Doctor," invited Thatcher Colt, in a color-less tone, after presenting him to the grim Dougherty and the particularly threatening Hogan.

The physician sank easily, almost with affected care-lessness, into a chair, and crossed his legs. Thatcher Colt began to question him with disarming mildness.

"You know that Geraldine Foster is dead?"

"I heard some talk while I was waiting outside. I gath-ered that she was murdered, the poor girl! But I have no details. Will you tell me how she was killed and where she was found?"

"Do you know anything about it at all?"

"No—certainly, no!"

"Haven't you any suspicions?"

"None," answered the doctor heartily.

"Where have you been since the night I talked to you in your office?"

"Away from New York."

"Where?"

"I was travelling in the West."

"When did you get back?"

"Two days ago."

"So you left town on Thursday, December 29, and re-turned on Thursday, January 5."

"Yes—two days ago, as I told you. But I have been vis-iting my father in Scarsdale. Tonight I returned home and found a detective who told me I should come here—that something had happened."

"Can you account for your time since your return?"

"Surely."

"Please do, then—here and now."

Maskell glanced with a superior air from Dougherty's red and frankly skeptical face to Hogan's shrewd, pale countenance, and then, with a sigh something akin to re-lief, he turned back to the Commissioner.

"I arrived in town early Thursday morning and went to my office. All day I was busy with my patients. But about three o'clock in the afternoon, I received a telephone call that gave me the shock of my life."

"From whom was that?"

"Mr. Colt," declared Doctor Maskell, his voice vibrating with a ring of conviction, "I talked with Geraldine Foster."

"Geraldine Foster!"

Dougherty's voice was a squeal of surprise. We were all astonished; the only person who seemed to regard it without emotion was the doctor himself.

"She said it was, and it sounded like her voice," he added calmly. "But the connection was bad."

"Go on," urged Colt. "What happened?"

"She informed me she was in some terrible trouble, but she could not tell me about it over the telephone, so she begged me to come to her at once, which I tried to do."

"You tried to do," snarled Hogan. "What did you do?"

"Geraldine asked me to meet her at the entrance of Bronx Park on the Pelham Parkway. I drove out there alone, parked near the entrance, waited two hours, and saw nothing of her. Then I came home."

"Did anybody who knew you see you there?" asked Thatcher Colt.

"Nobody, I am sorry to say."

"And when was this?"

"This was Thursday last, January 5, in the afternoon."

"The time she was murdered," thundered Dougherty. "And that is your alibi?"

"How does that affect me?" countered the doctor. But Thatcher Colt was not answering questions, he was asking them.

"You knew the police were looking for Geraldine Foster," he resumed. "Why didn't you come and tell me about that telephone call?"

"Geraldine told me she was in trouble of a private character. I wanted to talk with her first."

Dougherty snorted and winked at Hogan, as Colt veered to another tack.

"Doctor, you have an office in Washington Square and an apartment on Fifth Avenue. Do you rent or own any other property?"

"A good deal."

"Mind telling me where?"

Doctor Maskell then enumerated some farming land that he owned in upper New York State, a house on the West Side which he rented out, and a fishing shack down on the Eastern shore of Maryland.

"Well, but don't you and I both know that you also have a bungalow on Peddler's Road?"

Maskell was plainly taken aback at this.

"Right you are," he admitted. "I guessed you knew when I saw Mrs. Haberhorn. But why do you bring that up now?"

I noticed that a fugitive note of anxiety was in his voice.

"What did you use that house for—way off there in the woods?" asked Thatcher Colt.

Doctor Maskell cleared his throat, heavily.

"You needn't be embarrassed with me," pursued the Commissioner. "Did you have it as a hide-away for weekends that required privacy?"

Doctor Maskell shook his head.

"No. I hope that you do not assume—"

Thatcher Colt held up his hands in protest.

"I am not assuming anything, Doctor Maskell," he assured him. "Did you ever take Geraldine Foster to that place?"

"Absolutely never," said Doctor Maskell.

"Not even for a short visit?"

"Never."

"Did she know of its existence?"

"I—well, I don't think so."

The two men looked at each other in silence for a moment.

"Doctor," suddenly barked the Commissioner, "do you realize that you are in a nasty fix right about now?"

Maskell drew himself up with dignity.

"Will you tell me what my property on Peddler's Road has to do with all this?"

"Did you keep an axe on that place?"

"An axe?"

"Yes—a short handled axe, with a double blade."

"Why, yes, certainly, yes, I did."

"What did you use the axe for, Doctor Maskell?"

"For firewood."

"Nothing else?"

"What else?"

"Some one used it for something else, Doctor."

"I am not good at enigmas."

"Doctor Maskell, this is a fact—Geraldine Foster was murdered, hacked to pieces and the crime was done in your house and with your axe."

Doctor Maskell leaped to his feet. If he was acting it was magnificent.

"This is a trick," he shouted. "You are trying to scare me."

For reply, Thatcher Colt thrust near the man's face a photograph still wet, and showing the girl's nude body stiff in the grave.

All laughter was wiped away from the doctor's broad mouth as he glared at the print lying flat on his palms.

"Poor Geraldine," he muttered.

His voice grew stronger, his face crimson, as he turned on the Commissioner. "Who was the monster that would commit a crime like that—and on my property, my little house?"

"Never mind all that," snapped Thatcher Colt. "You must realize now that you have a lot to explain."

"When was she killed?" gasped Doctor Maskell, looking strangely around the room.

"I am asking the questions, Doctor."

"It does not matter. I shall prove my innocence."

"If you can do that, fine—in the face of what we can bring against you."

"Nevertheless," cried Doctor Maskell, "you will be unable to bring a single witness to place me on the scene of the murder. And surely some one will come forward to bear me out that I waited at the entrance to Bronx Park for a girl I believed to be alive! I am not afraid!"

As he was speaking, the door was opening and a patrolman stamped in with a sheaf of notes. Colt received them with unconcealed eagerness.

"Just a moment," he murmured. "These are the reports from the eight autopsies."

"Eight!" exclaimed Dougherty. "What do you mean—eight?"

"One girl, and seven pigeons," explained Colt. "Ah, and here is Doctor Multooler himself."

The Assistant Medical Examiner nodded wearily as he stood, just within the door, and wiped his glasses.

"How long had those pigeons been dead, Multooler?"

"At least ten days, sir," replied the Assistant Medical Examiner.

"The girl was supposed to be dead two days but the pigeons were dead ten days, eh?"

"Well, sir—we don't suppose that, any more."

"The autopsy changed your opinion?"

"Yes, it did," replied the Examiner. "Somebody tried to fool us. The girl had also been killed about ten days ago."

Thatcher Colt's face was very serious then, and he did not look at Doctor Maskell.

"Was there any food in her stomach?"

"Yes, sir."

"What food?"

"Snails."

"About how far digested?"

"Not more than five hours."

Thatcher Colt glanced around in brief accusing triumph.

"Then Geraldine Foster unquestionably met her death about five o'clock on the afternoon of December 24," he declared feelingly.

"Yes, sir."

"Thanks, Multooler."

"Yes—Sir!"

"Now—what did the chemist find in that bottle of water we took from the grave?"

"Tannic acid, sir. The body had been soaked in it, and a quart of it forced down the throat after death—the stomach was full of it."

"Tannic acid! Of course! Made from the bark of pine trees! Used in tanning leather, Dougherty. Tannic acid— that's what preserved the body. A clumsy trick! And an old one! It was used in the David S. Paul case, out in Tabernacle, New Jersey, but the police solved it in twenty-four hours. Why should this killer try that trick again?"

The Commissioner closed his eyes and remained silent. But Dougherty could seldom remain silent, and this was not one of the times.

"Colt," he exploded, in exasperation, "what in the name of Jesse James and the Seven Sutherland Sisters are you talking about? Hell, doesn't the District Attorney amount to anything around here?"

With a grateful smile, Thatcher Colt dismissed Multooler.

"It is very simple," he explained to the District Attorney. "Geraldine Foster was killed. Then she was put into
a bath-tub filled with water loaded with tannic acid and
that preserved the body."

"But why preserve the body?"

"It seems obvious enough. She was killed ten days ago,
but she was buried in the last forty-eight hours."

"I see!" cried Dougherty suddenly and loudly. Pushing
back his chair, he stood up, pounding his red fist into his
palm and striding back and forth. "It was a slick alibi."

"Dougherty, you're marvelous!" chuckled Thatcher Colt.

Not for a moment did the District Attorney discern the
sarcasm of his friend. His brain was rapidly sketching out
to him the wonderful possibilities now just made clear to
him.

"Why, it would be a perfect alibi," he repeated, glaring
at Doctor Maskell. "We are supposed to believe the murder
took place during the last 48 hours. And, of course, the
murderer hoped to account for his movements—I think
he's been stringing us here anyway. He thought he would
never be asked to show where he was when the murder
was really committed. Well, this is the crime of a genius,
Doctor Maskell—I'll leave it to you, only it didn't work."

"You're undoubtedly right, Mr. Dougherty," said Hogan.

"Bunk!" snorted Doctor Maskell.

The Commissioner laughed softly. It was like Dougherty, the hot-spur, to take another man's theory and in two
minutes come to believe it was his very own.

"My dear Mr. Dougherty," said Doctor Maskell boldly,
"don't you see that only a feeble-minded person would
think of such a scheme as that?"

"Feeble-minded? I think you consider yourself a
master mind," cried the District Attorney. "Our next job

is to find out who has bought a quantity of tannic acid recently."

Maskell ignored the last thrust.

"The alibi would be no good for the murderer for the last 48 hours, unless he had an accomplice," he assented. "Don't you realize somebody had to go up there and bury the body?"

"Well?"

"Well, that's as serious as if he did the murder. He was on the scene! It would take as much time to bury the body as it did to kill it—maybe more. So, such an alibi would be worthless to me or any one else."

But Dougherty was not to be out-faced by the calm reasoning of this baffling physician.

"Who would know about tannic acid, except you—a doctor? Who bought the muffler we found in the house? You— the doctor. By God, you're guilty," shouted Dougherty, leaping frantically to his feet. "Of course you're guilty!"

"You can't prove it," replied the doctor with determined calm. "On Christmas Eve I was distributing gifts to my patients. I was accompanied by my chauffeur and little Doris Morgan, who lives upstairs. For Christmas Eve I have a perfect alibi."

"Good!" said Thatcher Colt emphatically. "You have the rest of the night to prove it."

A haggard look crept across the face of Maskell.

"The third degree for me, eh?" he exclaimed, his eyes searching our faces. Hogan nodded. Dougherty nodded. Thatcher Colt nodded. Maskell forced a chuckle that seemed compounded of defiance, confidence or else great malevolence. I could not tell whether he was supremely brave or supremely cock-sure of himself. Balancing his weight from one foot to another, smiling, with his head turned to one side, and his hands in his pocket, he orated with strange and vital gusto:

"I am familiar with the confessions extorted by the French methods—the Parisian third degree. In fact, I have seen innocent men, at the Paris *Sûreté*, collapse into confession in the room that is called the Chamber of Spontaneous Avowals. The spontaneity of the avowals is accelerated by beating the soles of the bare feet of the unfortunate suspects with long staves. That is called the bastinado. Very well. The New York equivalent is probably a fist on the jaw. Nevertheless you will get nothing from me. I have an alibi. I did not kill Geraldine Foster."

"Alibi or ibi—just tell the truth. Mind?" asked Thatcher Colt.

"And if I do that I will have nothing to fear?"—mockingly.

"Except just what you said—a sock in the jaw," said Hogan, who had endured this exchange of compliments as long as he could.

He seized the doctor by the arm. But the latter continued to address Thatcher Colt.

"I was called away from a minor operation to come down here," he complained. "I have partaken of nothing but the salted roe of the sturgeon and a cocktail, just after the operation, since luncheon. Might I have a sandwich before Hogan and his friends begin to entertain me?"

"No," growled Hogan. "Step lively. There's a gang waiting for you in a room downstairs, and it's been a long time since they had any exercise."

At the threshold, the doctor glanced back at the three of us.

"It's terrible, what can happen to a man through force of circumstances," he remarked. "However, I don't mind, Mr. Commissioner."

"We will see you before you have your breakfast," promised Thatcher Colt, his face inscrutable.

Then Hogan joggled the arm of his prisoner and led him hurriedly down an inner corridor.

"A hundred to one that fellow breaks before morning," said Dougherty.

But Thatcher Colt only smiled.

10
A LONG, LONG NIGHT

Doctor Maskell was subjected to the ordeal of a third degree that is still considered a classic in Headquarters.

He was not under arrest, although there was more than sufficient evidence to hold him under a short affidavit, or to jail him in the House of Detention as a material witness. No forcible persuasion was necessary; he willingly consented to the almost inhuman treatment to which he was now exposed. Of course, a man of Maskell's standing was in no danger of beating from the police. Nor by this do I mean to pretend that physical violence is no longer practiced. It is still practiced, although not as much as before. But such treatment is reserved for men who will respond to nothing else, who are themselves violent creatures intimidated by nothing except violent physical pain. Moreover, the results from such manhandling are no longer so effective in court. A prisoner roughly treated in the third degree can call his lawyer the next day, exhibit his bruises, have them photographed, and the pictures of the wounds will be shown at the trial to discredit his enforced revelations. The chief value lies in getting a confession that can be substantiated by confirming details subsequently checked up. With men of the stamp of Doctor Maskell, the police have more subtle methods; before the night was over Doctor Maskell was sure to wish that physical violence was all he had to face.

Hogan led the suspect downstairs to a brightly lighted office, where a battalion of questioners awaited him. The attack upon him began at once, launched by three of the most experienced men in the Department. But the dark hours passed and a calm man, with ready answers, still faced the onslaught of hard and snarling investigators, grimly intent on a breakdown. At 3 a.m., when Thatcher Colt, Dougherty and I joined them, they had got nowhere. They could not seem to break this man's iron nerve. Maskell had answered all their questions over and over again and not once had they tripped him. Often he smiled at them in his irritatingly superior manner. True, he was possessed of a higher degree of mentality than most of his questioners, but they had the strength of numbers, of reserve force, brutally marshalled against him. First, one detective would question him for fifteen minutes, then leave and another would begin, while the first checked up on any doubtful information the doctor had given him. During the night at least a dozen detectives from the Deputy Inspector down, bullied and harassed the man with trick questions. At five o'clock, when they gave Maskell a glass of milk and a sandwich, his story was still unbroken. It was one of the most desperate attempts to break down a denial in my experience in the Department. Outside the door of the examination room, two newspaper men had dragged a table from the Criminal Identification Bureau and sat there, playing "Seven-up" and making side bets on the result. When we led Doctor Maskell out of the office and took him to the washroom, one of the reporters remarked that the doctor appeared to be standing the ordeal of grilling much better than his tormentors. We took him back, and then the Commissioner again took charge.

First Thatcher Colt reasoned with him. Over and over again he took him through his story, but Maskell stuck to his single yarn without the slightest significant change, recounting the hours at which he had delivered the presents, his return to his office, the interview with the mysterious woman, his dinner later in a restaurant of the Fifth Avenue Hotel. At six o'clock in the morning, Doctor Maskell was still far from being a broken man. His energy was equal to Thatcher Colt's restless vitality. Finally, Dougherty stepped to the fore, whispered into the ear of Thatcher Colt, and the Commissioner nodded in skeptical acquiescence.

"Now, Doctor," proposed Dougherty, "I want you to come with me."

Thus it was that in the dark hours of that morning, Dougherty, followed by Colt and myself, motored Doctor Humphrey Maskell to the Morgue, at Bellevue Hospital, Twenty-sixth Street and East River. He walked into the building like a man led into an ambuscade. There he was confronted with the body. At this dreadful sight, Doctor Maskell could not remain unmoved. He betrayed signs of nervousness and repulsion. But who could say they were indication of fear or guilt? Finally the police brought him back to the examination room, with no admission drawn from his stern lips. They were weary, all of them, with the night's inquisition, but secretly they marveled at the strength, the energy, the undaunted vitality of their prisoner.

Meanwhile, detectives were checking up on all the stories that he told. It was at this time that Thatcher Colt had a long and whispered conference with Merle Dougherty, and a messenger was dispatched to the building in which the doctor maintained his offices.

But Thatcher Colt was not ready to give up. He knew that when all seemed lost, victory might be within a hand's

reach. Again, and still again, he made Doctor Maskell re-
tell his story. He was resorting to the oldest and one of
the most effective devices known to the operating police
of the world—the trapping effect of repetition. Make the
suspect tell the same story often enough, in wearying repetition, until he is sick of the very lies that he is telling,
and eventually, often, I think by the sheer rebellion of the
outraged subconscious, he lets fall some significant little
detail which, seized upon and followed up, may break his
story altogether. That was what Thatcher Colt was hoping
to do with Maskell. He tried to reach him from a different
angle.

"Do you believe in justice, Doctor Maskell?"

"Yes."

"Do you believe in God—or, let us say, a Supreme Being?"

"Yes," he replied boldly.

"And do you want to see justice done in this case?"

"Yes, certainly. But what is justice?"

Upon this, Thatcher Colt criticized him bitterly. He
told him he was overbearing and conceited. Most of the
people who knew him disliked him, and the Commissioner
told him so. That did begin to get under the suspect's
skin. Maskell wanted to be popular—and he never had
been unpopular. The dislike of people affected him pain-
fully. So Thatcher Colt harped on that.

"If you want to know how you stand," the Commissioner
told him, "you let me call Betty Canfield in here. She will
tell you quickly enough. She believes you chopped up that
beautiful girl with an axe."

Maskell paled, but made no answer. Dougherty, springing forward, shook his finger in his face and cried:

"Here is what will happen to you, Doctor. I'll try you
in court and you'll be found guilty, sure as hell. For a
short time you will be in a cell at Sing Sing. In the death

house. On the last day, they will shave your head and slit your trousers. You will begin your last earthly walk. On one side will be a chaplain, praying for your soul. On the other will be a guard.

"A small crowd will be waiting there to see Doctor Maskell go to death for the murder of Geraldine Foster. When that time comes, Doc—go in like a man. I'm not promising you anything. Even if you confess, and save me a lot of trouble. I can't get you anything less than a sentence of death. You are going to be electrocuted, because you're guilty. That's final. So why don't you take your medicine like a man? If you don't, remember one thing—I'm going to be in that audience and I'm going to be close enough to kick you in the face."

Doctor Maskell's features registered distaste. He stood up and began pacing around in a twelve-foot circle, and for a moment I thought his collapse was near. But no, he was still in thorough command of himself, though he looked a bit weary when a new detail of smiling well-slept detectives came in to take over the job of questioning him.

No one but Thatcher Colt knew how long this grim inquisition would proceed and the Commissioner was keeping his own counsel. At cock-crow, they were still at it and the doctor was undaunted. The Commissioner sent me back to the typewriter to transcribe my notes.

Dawn in Centre Street! What little of aura the break of day ever lets fall upon Police Headquarters came through my window and lay pinkly on my typewriter. Presently, while I was pounding away at the keys, the sleepless Captain Henry came in with the astonishing announcement that some indignant kinfolk of Doctor Maskell were demanding to see the Commissioner at once. They were Mr. and Mrs. George Maskell, the criminal lawyer and his wife.

11
THICKER THAN WATER

Ever since my old reporting days on the Sun I had known George Maskell and admired him for the good-hearted and sentimental buccaneer that he was. Like Arthur Garfield Hays and Clarence Darrow, the brother of the man we now suspected of murder was a rank sentimentalist. He trained with a clever group of skeptical thinkers, laughed at the Humanists, considered himself a sophisticate, while being naive and sentimental enough to believe that the oppressed and the down-trodden have claims on human consideration and a right to simple justice, the latter being one of the myths in which these charming emotionalists still believe. Although no longer in active practice, George Maskell is still bright in the memories of New Yorkers. At the time of the Geraldine Foster case he was one of the most picturesque figures in the affairs of the community. Already a rich lawyer, and half-heir to his father's considerable fortune, he espoused all the radical causes where he felt that an issue of justice was involved. George Maskell has sometimes been called a Robin Hood among the lawyers, for he served rich corporations and charged them enormous fees but made no charge to the poor radicals whose cases he took.

This fondness for radicals had not made him any too popular in the Police Department, although Thatcher Colt always admired George Maskell.

As this vital and picturesque figure was ushered into
Thatcher Colt's private office, I was again reminded of
my chief's description of him, made some years ago—"A
man with the face of an old war horse." He resembled
his brother almost not at all. The criminal lawyer was a
short man, with a bald head, a shrewd face, wrinkles of
thought in his forehead and furrows in his cheeks. Only
in his eyes was there a likeness to the laughing physician
of Washington Square. As he came through the private
door, I noticed the same twinkle, or gleam, or glitter, of
inscrutability in those hazel eyes. Although the hour was
scarcely more than six o'clock, he was exquisitely attired
in grey trousers, and a long-tailed coat, stiff shirt, a high
stand-up collar and flowing black tie that gave him an
old-fashioned, out-moded, almost a ministerial air.

He smiled at me as he entered, but already my eyes had
fled from his familiar face to study his companion. That
was the first time I had ever seen Natalie Maskell. Often
I had read of her, and listened to reporters' yarns, told
in speakeasies. Her beauty had been variously reported.
I remember that in one place in Forty-eighth Street, near
Sixth Avenue, a free-for-all started during the trial of the
Albany checkmen—the famous forgers that George Maskell convicted, when called in as special counsel by the
District Attorney. But it was not over this famous forgery
case that the reporters fought, but whether Natalie Maskell's dimple was on the right cheek or the left. The one
thing agreed upon in all quarters was that Natalie Maskell,
in spite of her beauty, had one of the best legal minds before the bar. She and her husband were inseparable.

As he stood aside to permit her to answer, I rose and
made them welcome. She was tall, pale and august—a
woman with dark-red hair and lovely features, commanding in her softness and charm and with tragic eyes that
seemed to have received unspeakable confessions. I do not

think I have ever seen a sadder or more beautiful woman. She looked around inquiringly, and then her eyes came back to me, standing beside the desk of Thatcher Colt. I explained that I feared it was impossible to see either the Police Commissioner or the District Attorney at this time. Nodding sagely, George Maskell blew his nose, making a sound like the whinny of a horse.

"Nevertheless, they'll see me," he said confidently, his voice thick, husky and yet not unpleasant. "You tell the Commissioner I've come here to sit alongside of my brother while he is being questioned."

"Did Doctor Maskell send for you?" I inquired.

At this piece of impertinence, as they might have chosen to regard it, George Maskell looked at his wife with eyes that seemed to hold a conversation in a secret language. It was only my imagination, over-wrought, I suppose, after the long and weary night, but George Maskell always impressed me as a superior and mysterious being, this George who in his legal work went from one courtroom to another, from cell to death house and back again to the pure air of sidewalks, invariably accompanied by this beautiful woman, this lovely adviser at his side.

More, it seemed to me that George had conveyed to his wife, without speech, the suggestion that she, better than he, could prevail over an impressionable young man like myself.

"No, my brother-in-law did not send for us," she explained, with a friendly smile. "Mr. Maskell and I were starting off very early this morning on an auto tour to Florida. We bought the papers on the ferry, read about Doctor Maskell, and came right back."

One could not resist the gentle and earnest manner of Natalie Maskell. I do not regard myself as an impressionable person, but it did seem to me that it would be no more than my duty to let Thatcher Colt know they were in his office. I was just about to buzz for Captain Henry when the door opened and my chief came in, followed by Dougherty.

Briskly enough, Thatcher Colt walked in, with Dougherty, blotch-eyed and weary, trudging behind him. I could tell from the slump of the District Attorney's shoulders that Maskell had not confessed. But at the sight of the other attorney and his beautiful companion, Dougherty straightened up and fumbled at his tie.

There was a moment's exchange of greetings and then George Maskell demanded to see his brother.

"Now, George, you know we can't do that just now," protested Dougherty. I have noticed that all lawyers like to call each other by their first names, especially climbers like Dougherty when they meet famous men like George Maskell.

"Why not? Is he arrested?"

"Doctor Maskell is not under arrest," explained Thatcher Colt, lifting a nose-gay from a glass of water and sniffing it. "He is merely being questioned."

"But, Mr. Commissioner, why do you try to put this crime on him?"

Thatcher Colt replied that some of the circumstances had not been explained to the satisfaction of the police.

"Humphrey is quite innocent of any crime," declared George Maskell, "and I would appreciate it if you would let him know that we are here."

Thatcher Colt leaned across the desk and looked the lawyer squarely in the eye.

"I have always understood," he said, "that you did not approve of your brother!"

"In a time like this, blood is thicker than water," replied George Maskell, with a gleam in his eyes.

Natalie Maskell took an impulsive step forward.

"Mayn't we leave him a note, at least?" she entreated, and Dougherty made her a gallant bow. Her husband sat in Colt's chair and scribbled hastily on a scratch pad:

"We are standing behind you. Send for us when you want us.
      "George and Natalie and Dad."

No one spoke while the lawyer was writing, but Thatcher Colt seemed very nervous. He walked up and down the room, like a man possessed with impatience, resenting an intrusion. Suddenly he reached on a high shelf and pulled down two file boxes of old correspondence, raising a cloud of filthy dust at which Dougherty shouted indignantly. I must confess that I had never seen my chief perform so awkwardly. He was full of apologies, but Dougherty's face was discolored with dust, and Mrs. Maskell needed all the resources of her feminine arsenal to repair the ravages.

"I found it!" exclaimed Thatcher Colt, after opening the first file box. "Here is the letter of congratulation I wrote you, Mr. Maskell, on the Scopes trial. You never replied to it."

"Damned careless of me," said George Maskell, with a bleak glance. Indeed, the curious behavior of the Police Commissioner had perplexed us all. But there was no further apology from Colt, as with great dignity, the Maskells took their departure. The minute the door closed, Dougherty picked up his hat and threw it up into the air. After this undignified act, he exclaimed:

"What a trial this will be! Brother fighting for brother—but I will beat him, Colt—this is one time that all the genius of George Maskell, and all the prettiness of his wife looking tragically toward the jury box, shall not avail to cheat justice."

"Oh, stop making speeches, for the love of God," said Thatcher Colt.

At that moment, Hogan threw open the door and led Doctor Maskell into the office. The prisoner was haggard, disheveled, his clothing disarrayed, but his eyes still indomitable.

"Did I see my brother down the hall?" he demanded, looking at Colt.

The Commissioner told him frankly what had happened, greatly to Dougherty's disgust, I am afraid. More, the Commissioner added that from the far window of the office Maskell could see his callers in their car, still standing outside of Police Headquarters.

"I would like to get at least a glimpse of Natalie," said the doctor, with a strange glance at the Commissioner.

"Come to this window," said Colt, ignoring Dougherty's glare. "There she is in the seat behind the wheel."

For a long, thoughtful moment, Doctor Humphrey Maskell stared down at his sister-in-law. Some powerful emotion, more moving and more troubling than all the dark questions hurled at him during the night, possessed his singular glances through that window. I found myself wondering. Did the doctor love the beautiful Natalie Maskell? Was it because of her that the brothers had quarreled? And then came the incredible suspicion—could a woman have done this awful crime? Was there an illicit love-affair between these two? Was Natalie Maskell jealous of Geraldine Foster? I admit these speculations were untrue, unfounded and fantastic, but they show the uncertain state of mind, the unfixed nature of my suspicions, at this stage of the game.

"Now," said Thatcher Colt, suddenly breaking the silence, "my dear doctor, I have taken the liberty of making some arrangements for our morning."

"Yes, certainly," said Doctor Maskell, turning from the window with a deep sigh.

"There is another car downstairs, in which you will find some of your friends. We are going on a journey."

"Without breakfast?" asked the physician.

"I am afraid so," replied the Commissioner, while Dougherty laughed, shook hands with my chief and promised to see him later in the day. Then he and Hogan departed, leaving the next stage of the investigation in our hands.

"If you think that extra little torment will help in breaking my nerves," said the doctor, "let me disabuse your mind. I have eaten no breakfast, except hot water, in twenty years, and, as a doctor, staying up all night is no great strain on me."

We descended into the fresh air of the young morning. At dawn, there had been a sun, but already banks of rain-clouds were massing in the heavens; the air was damp and cold; it was the beginning, after an hour's interlude, of another spell of dismal and cheerless weather.

In front of 240 Centre Street a maroon-colored Auburn car was drawn up at the curb, with that strange little fellow Checkles sitting at the wheel.

My chief explained to me, in an aside, that the Inspector and some of the men had been talking with Checkles. The best they could get out of him was that he was with the doctor all through Christmas Eve afternoon. Beside Checkles in the car, smiling a little wanly, and as pale as a moon at dawn, Doctor Maskell took his place. Then he looked back and in the rear seat, he saw a woman and a child. The mother, I recognized as Felise Morgan, and the little girl was Doris Morgan, the child companion of Doctor Maskell, his living alibi. She was quite pretty. Later I learned that she was ten years old. Her golden hair and

large blue eyes and colorful dress and hat gave her a rather
spoiled and stagey air—one would expect her to grow up
into a cinema star, if cinema stars ever do grow up. But
what interested me most was the love and tenderness in
Doctor Maskell's eyes when he looked at little Doris. I
think the sight of her quite unmanned him. He caught her
to him as she rose with a squeal of joy at sight of him, and
she kissed him in lively, intimate and trusting fashion.

"Helloa, Doris! Helloa, Checkles," called the Commissioner, taking his place beside the child and motioning me
to a folding seat in front of him.

"Good mornings and good nights and good fellows and
good gods," said Checkles, his head bent over the wheel of
the car, and he pushed the horn button in the middle of
the wheel with his long, peaked nose so that the car cried
out as if in fright at his behavior.

Doris laughed.

"Isn't Checkles too funny for words?" she asked, with a
grown-up glance at Thatcher Colt. "He always blows the
horn with his nose."

The Commissioner nodded, as he drew a slip of paper
from his pocket, and read off the names and addresses of
the patients of Doctor Maskell to whom, so the suspect
declared, he and Doris and Checkles had delivered the
presents.

"All correct," said Maskell.

Then we further delayed our start while the Commissioner talked earnestly with Doris. He told her she was a
very important person, and that she could help the great
City of New York and she must try to remember everything she could. She promised with the most grown-up
and gracious smile imaginable.

"You were with the doctor every part of the time on
Christmas Eve?" asked Commissioner Colt.

"Yes, sir, every part," said Doris Morgan firmly.

"Now," continued Thatcher Colt, "according to my memorandum, you went first to an address on Patchin Place. Is that right?"

"Yes, certainly," replied the doctor in a hoarse voice. Colt gave Checkles his orders and immediately we started zigzagging up and across town, in the direction of Greenwich Village. Whenever it was necessary to blow the horn, I noticed, with extreme distaste, that Checkles bent forward and pushed the round, black button with his nose. There was no conversation during that journey, until we reached the narrow impasse behind the Jefferson Market Court, where, for many years, artists and poets have lived in the little red brick houses, rejoicing in the tiny trees, the narrow sidewalks, and the general air of another century that hovers over the place.

"Doris," said Thatcher Colt, "do you remember anything about your last visit here?"

"Oh, yes," said the child. "We brought a parcel, done up in paper and ribbon, to an old lady who lives in that third house over there."

"Who delivered the package?"

"The doctor went to the door and rang the bell and the click came to the little door and he sent me up to deliver it."

"How long did that take?"

"Oh, not more than a second or so. The doctor told me I mustn't loiter, because we had so many other places to go. I was awful tired by the time we got home."

As we started off again, Thatcher Colt began to question Mrs. Morgan.

"You were an intimate friend of Geraldine Foster?"

"Oh, no. Our apartment is over the doctor's office. Doris and Geraldine met in the halls. They became friendly. The doctor took a fancy to Doris and soon we all got to know each other."

We fully understood the weariness of little Doris before we had finished that twisting and traffic-tormented
itinerary. In and out of the crowded New York streets we
drove, while Checkles pushed the horn button with his
nose, and heaped maledictions on taxi drivers and pedestrians who tempted death under our wheels. From house
to house we drove, from a broker in East Twelfth Street, to
an actor who lived at the Chelsea Hotel. Farther north we
were slowly creeping on our journey, which was confined
largely to the West Side, but by the time we had stopped
in front of the Sherman Square Hotel, Doctor Maskell
reminded us that it was just three o'clock on Christmas
Eve afternoon that he had been there before. He knew by
the fact that he had inquired the time of the doorman,
wondering if he would be able to complete the rest of his
trips before it was time for Doris to be back in her home.
The doorman knew the doctor, who often called to visit
one patient, a retired merchant tailor who lived on the
eighth floor of the hotel. When questioned, the doorman
perfectly recalled Doctor Maskell asking the time and he
further recollected that it was three o'clock.

As we drove past the barren Shakespeare Garden in
Central Park, I had to tell myself that so far the doctor's
alibi had been consistently sustained. Then, at the next
place we stopped, a small hotel apartment house near Central Park, we came upon a surprising piece of information.
The patient to whom Doctor Maskell had delivered a present there was a Mrs. Westock. She told the Commissioner
that, on Christmas Eve, before the doctor reached her
house, someone had called on her telephone and asked for
the physician.

"It was a woman's voice," said Mrs. Westock. "She
seemed to be very anxious for me to get word to him. The
message she left was: 'Please come at once to Peddler's
Road. Something terrible has happened.'"

"She did not leave any name?"

"No, sir. Nor her telephone number."

"Did you give the doctor the message?"

"Yes, sir."

"What did he say?"

"He looked surprised, but all he said was 'Thanks.'"

This conversation took place in the Westock apartment, and naturally Doctor Maskell did not hear it, for he remained in the car with Detective Burke guarding the whole party. Thatcher Colt did not tell the doctor about Mrs. Westock's story. Soon the car had crossed Fifth Avenue, continuing east until Park Avenue, where finally we stopped in front of a large apartment house.

"Oh," exclaimed Doris, "here is where I had the ice-cream."

Thatcher Colt had his hand on the door, but at this remark, he settled back and looked gravely down at Doris. Watching Maskell, I saw that he did seem concerned.

"Where did you have ice-cream, Doris?" asked the Commissioner, casually.

"Checkles and I had ice-cream while Doctor Maskell delivered some presents by himself," answered Doris.

"Where?"

"Right there!"

The child pointed out of the car window to a confectioner's on the opposite corner.

"Did you have more than one plate of ice-cream?" asked Thatcher Colt.

"Three! I had three!" cried Checkles gloatingly, as he turned and looked at us over his shoulder. "But Doris is a lady and took only one. She had to wait for me, though—I had three."

Thatcher Colt closed his eyes. I could almost follow the rapid calculations he was making in the isolation of blindness that he loved to impose upon his vision when he was thinking quickly. Perhaps Checkles and the child had been left in the place long enough—I could see the dangerous implications of this disclosure. When Thatcher Colt opened his eyes, I could also see that he had his finger on the first weak link in the chain of Doctor Maskell's perfect alibi.

"What were you doing, Doctor, when they were in the confectioner's?" he asked point-blank.

"I distributed seven presents in the neighborhood," replied the doctor promptly.

"That's right," said Doris innocently. "He wasn't here when we were finished eating—we had to wait for him a long, long time."

Again Thatcher Colt closed his eyes and considered the importance of this anachronism. "We had to wait for him a long, long time,"—I could almost see the lightning of calculation, suspicion, leaping and flashing across the stormy sky of the Commissioner's thoughts.

For what reason we did not as yet know, Geraldine had gone to the house on Peddler's Road. From there she might have telephoned Mrs. Westock. This seemed all the more credible because only Geraldine would know all the places the doctor was planning to visit, and how to reach him. In answer to her summons, he might have left Checkles and Doris in the confectioner's and rushed off to kill her and get back. It was close figuring—but it could have been done. Such at least was the theory, inevitably suggested by this startling gap just disclosed in the doctor's itinerary.

And still the doctor smiled, as if, telepathically, he knew what was passing in the Commissioner's mind, and mine, smiling as if he exulted and rejoiced because he knew there was still something missing, before they could bind him to the crime.

"There are only seven more addresses on your list," remarked Thatcher Colt. "Were the seven presents you told us about the last?"

"Yes," said Doctor Maskell. "From here we went home."

"Can any one identify you as having delivered these seven presents?"

"No. By that time I was late. I was hurried. I merely dropped them on hall tables. I saw no one."

"Yet you took an hour to deliver them?"

"I do not know how much time I took."

"Well, you must know this blows your alibi to smithereens."

Without another word, Thatcher Colt then sent Mrs. Morgan and Doris home in a taxicab. Burke went with them, agreeing to meet the Commissioner at Police Headquarters later in the afternoon.

"No, Checkles," said the Commissioner, "drive us up to the house on Peddler's Road."

Checkles laughed, a low-pitched chortle of laughter, as he punched the auto siren with his nose and pulled the lever into gear.

"Peddler's Road!" he chuckled. "Whew!"

I have seen a suspected man look down upon the scene of a crime, and remain quite unmoved; not by the quiver of a muscle or the flicker of a lash did he betray emotion. Yet that man was guilty. But I have also seen a suspected, really innocent man go into hysterics at the sight of a butchered body. The hysterical man was innocent, although he actually confessed to the crime.

This may make the whole process of "confrontation and return" seem a waste of time, but in a sufficient number of instances, a criminal cannot endure to look again upon his work. Often enough to make it worth while, he shrieks out his guilt at the top of his voice and gives all the needed confirming details.

It was not, as Thatcher Colt explained to me later, with any hope of unnerving the doctor by horror, that we were taking him back to Peddler's Road. Instead, my chief had the idea that some sentimental remembrance might unexpectedly upset the poise of Maskell—another onslaught on human nature, through emotion.

All the paths approaching Peddler's Road had been roped off and put under guard, and crowds of baffled and morbidly curious persons strained against the ropes around the base of the hill. Inside, reporters were buzzing and snooping for clues, and it seemed to me as if there were plainclothes men and patrolmen behind every tree. The search for clues was still going forward relentlessly.

Avoiding the crowds by approaching from the rear, we climbed the hill and as we approached the house, Thatcher Colt said to Maskell:

"You know, Doctor, when we found the body, it had a pillow case over the head, as if the murderer could not bear to look upon the dead face, after what he had done."

"Yes, certainly?" said Doctor Maskell, in a tone of inquiry.

"It was a pillow case with silken rosebuds embroidered on it. I could not find its mate in your bungalow. Do you happen to know what happened to the other one?"

"I know nothing of that," replied Doctor Maskell disdainfully.

"Ah, well," said Thatcher Colt, "eventually we will find out about that pillow case. Come in!"

The doctor removed his hat as he entered the door of his own little house. One glance at his face showed me that he was profoundly moved. He looked at the disorder, and at the detectives still searching in the house—they had been there all night and they were still there, ferreting everywhere, the same area gone over three times by three different men—Colt was resolved that nothing should be lost. Maskell held his hat before his heart and looked miserably upon the wreckage, the carnage, the red stains.

"You can see, Doctor," said Thatcher Colt quietly, "that a great deal of blood was spilled. It spilled through the open trapdoor to the fireplace floor, and pooled in a hollow by the kitchen door. Isn't it extraordinary, how much blood there really is in a human body, Doctor Maskell? Your dissection practice partly prepared you for that, of course—but when you start to let it run out of a living person, there's a lot of it, isn't there, Doctor—like a red Niagara coming from sweet young veins and arteries."

Maskell was about to light a cigarette, but Thatcher Colt, with his hand on his shoulder, commanded his attention, and his eyes required an answer.

"Thatcher Colt," said Doctor Maskell, "I shall have to listen to you but my mind cannot be shocked into a breakdown, or fake confession, or anything else."

"No," agreed Colt. "The forthright, downright, outright methods of a simple policeman like myself may seem very crude to your preconceived notions of how this thing should be done. But I do know one thing—that reason is the certain method that can appeal to you, Doctor."

"Right!" agreed Maskell.

"You know there is a perfect case against you."

"I have been told that."

"Opportunity."

"No. I had no opportunity to do all this."

"Where were you, then, when Checkles and Doris were eating their ice-cream?"

"I told you."

"You told me a cock-and-bull story. Do you expect any jury to believe that?"

Instead of replying the doctor was looking mournfully around the room.

"I can't believe it!" he murmured.

"Neither will the jury," snapped Colt, accepting the *non-sequitur* as a reply.

"Ah, haven't we talked enough? Do as you please—only let me have some sleep now," cried Maskell with a shudder.

But Thatcher Colt only shook his head.

"The police won't sleep until we get our man," he replied.

Doctor Maskell forced a smile, and an unearthly chuckle.

"Trying the methods of the Spanish Inquisition?" he mocked. "No sleep for a suspected man, eh? Gentlemen—I shall be awake when you are all nodding and snoring. I am a doctor—and I never sleep when a patient needs me."

And he smiled mockingly.

12

THE LIE DETECTOR

Upon the orders of Thatcher Colt, I was sent home to snatch a few hours' sleep before another long night of inquisition that loomed ahead. However, I did not feel like sleep, but spent the late hours of the afternoon being bathed and shaved, and then having tea with Betty Canfield. Every time we broke bread together, we liked each other better. In the course of our connection, she assured me her engagement to Bruce was never really serious and was all ended now.

With a light heart, I returned to Headquarters. It was five o'clock when I reached the Commissioner's office where I found Thatcher Colt in deep conversation with Dougherty. Neither the District Attorney nor my chief had been in their beds since the case "broke", as we used to phrase it in the city room. There were no signs of weariness on either of their faces, nor did it seem to me that Dougherty's arrogance was in the smallest degree lessened.

From their conversation, I learned that Doctor Maskell had been permitted a few hours' sleep in his apartment, with a policeman guarding his doors. Meanwhile, Bruce Foster had returned to Headquarters and Thatcher Colt had drawn from him a complete statement of his movements—the details of which were easily and simply

checked and seemed to furnish him with a clear exonera-
tion from all suspicion. At this time, Colt and Dougherty
both regarded Bruce as eliminated from the case. The District Attorney went further and declared that Armstrong,
too, was above suspicion. But with this, Thatcher Colt
would not agree.

"There is a theory that may involve Armstrong," he
declared.

"Why don't you spill the theory to me?" demanded
Dougherty.

"Because you would disbelieve in it so much you might
even block me from then on," said Colt. "No—give us the
rest of this day, Dougherty."

"I promised until midnight," sighed Dougherty. "And
while I have all the evidence in the world to justify the
arrest of Maskell, I'll live up to my word. The doctor is
guilty as red-fire hell. Why don't you give up the agree-
ment and let me go ahead?"

"I believe," replied Thatcher Colt, "that before midnight, you will agree with me that there is something much
more surprising yet to be found."

Dougherty groaned with an air of conscious Christian
fortitude.

"All right," he growled. "Where do we go from here?"

Thatcher Colt stood up, smiling mysteriously. "To the
private dwelling of the Police Commissioner of the City of
New York," he divulged. "There we will get the truth out
of Humphrey Maskell."

Dougherty looked his astonishment. Thatcher Colt's
proposal seemed incomprehensible to him then, and, indeed, to me, too. Why should we have to examine Doctor
Maskell in the home of the Commissioner? Why not at
Police Headquarters, where we could have information,
check-ups, all the aid we needed? The District Attorney

shrugged his shoulders and gave his famulus, Hogan, a significant ogle as we left the office and descended to the street. Soon we were uptown, in the new Bohemia of the West Side, the neighborhood between the Verdi and Dante triangles—near which was the home of the Commissioner. He lived in a modest house in the West Seventies; there were flower boxes before the windows, and bright green paint on the woodwork; it was much more like a house in some dozing little Southern city than in the heart of Manhattan. Thatcher Colt had lived for many years in that house. In fact, he was born in another of the houses on the same block, just across from No. 244, where Elwell, the bridge expert, was mysteriously murdered. Some day I shall describe the singular rooms contained in that quiet and pretty little dwelling—the weapons' chamber, the room where Thatcher Colt conducted his own original researches into "ballistics", his poison room—but all these things played their parts in the detection of subsequent crimes. Tonight we were led to the library of Thatcher Colt—a vast, immense room running the entire stretch of one hundred and fifty feet on the third floor, and shelving a personally selected collection of more than fifteen thousand books on crime and its related topics, more than half of which would not be found together in any ordinary library in the world.

Waving us to comfortable chairs, Thatcher Colt retired. Dougherty and Hogan looked around them with an air of suspicion and bewilderment. Their very glances seemed to say that Thatcher Colt could not be a practical man, with all those books in his possession. Presently, the Commissioner reappeared, wearing a dressing gown of strong, rich silk, a flowered paduasoy. From a covered recess in the library wall, a small alcove above a table, he drew out a tray on which reposed glasses, and a bottle of old port.

Withdrawing the cork, he called our attention to a filmy crust of scales of tartar on the top, the beeswing of a rare old wine.

"In this xerophilous land," said Thatcher Colt, "there is not much more wine like this. Gentlemen, your health!"

We all felt very solemn and important as we drank that precious liquor. It warmed the inner lining of my soul. Then, leaning back in his chair, Thatcher Colt, resumed:

"I must begin by explaining to you that this is wholly an extra-legal proceeding. I must also make that perfectly clear to Maskell. He has the right to decline to have anything to do with these experiments."

"What kind of bunk have you fallen for, Thatcher Colt?" As he asked the question, Dougherty almost hummed the words, while his hands, spread out on his knees, seemed itching to get hold of Maskell and pitch him into a cell.

"Two things," replied the Commissioner, "the first is this!"

On a table, at his right hand, was an object covered with a cloth of green serge. Lifting this, Colt disclosed an odd affair, a drum-like electrical instrument.

"What in hell is that?" mocked Dougherty, his hands in his pockets, as he leaned over at a rakish angle and surveyed the machine quizzically.

"It is called a pneumo-cardio-sphygmometer," answered Thatcher Colt.

Dougherty blinked in over-done astonishment at his friend. The District Attorney was a well-educated man, but for so long had he cultivated his public pose of roughness and readiness that he had almost convinced himself he was an illiterate.

"A what, Mr. Commissioner?" he purred, with such unction that I was sure he regretted the absence of an audience to laugh at his comedy.

"It is commonly called a lie detector," explained Thatcher Colt.

Dougherty clapped his hands together and laughed immoderately.

"Have you fallen for that piffle?" he cried. "My God, you'll be using New Thought on your prisoners next. What is the Police Department of the City of New York coming to, I want to know?"

Thatcher Colt remained imperturbable.

"You are in ignorance of the facts, Dougherty," he remonstrated quietly. "This machine is in almost daily use in the Illinois State Penitentiary at Joliet. Moreover, it is employed by the police of many other cities—it has been used in more than five thousand criminal cases in the Berkeley, California, Police Department alone."

Dougherty sniffed in audible contempt.

"Whoever got up such a fool machine as that?" he asked, shaking his head heavily.

"It is the invention of one of my old friends, Captain August Vollmer."

"I've heard mention of *him* somewhere," conceded Dougherty.

"No doubt. Captain Vollmer is one of the foremost criminologists in the country. He was the Police Advisory Expert on President Hoover's Commission on Law Observance and Enforcement. He is also a Professor of Criminology at the University of Chicago. Captain Vollmer has told me, more than once, that he has never seen a real failure in the use of this amazing instrument."

Dougherty again shook his head, staunchly refusing to be impressed. But his curiosity was aroused.

"How does the fool thing work?" he asked.

Thatcher Colt lifted a set of leather-covered plates on a chain and Dougherty studied them attentively.

"These plates enclose the suspect's chest," explained the Commissioner. "And this rubber tube goes around the arm. Both lead to the drum there, to which electric writing pens are attached. Then you question the suspect. His reactions to your questions, that is, his respiration and blood pressure, are registered by the pens on ruled paper from a revolving drum roll within the box. This makes a complete graph or chart of the suspect's emotional reactions under questioning."

Dougherty made a comical face.

"I don't like these new-fangled notions."

"It's not new-fangled," answered Colt patiently. "The lie detector was first used for criminological purposes more than twenty years ago. But that was only the heartbeat,—the blood-pressure record is more recent."

"And you actually think this contraption will help us in breaking the tale of Doctor Maskell?"

"It will get us the truth," insisted Thatcher Colt. "I have no hesitation in saying that I consider this little box, and the other invention which we may have to use later tonight on the doctor, the two greatest steps forward in criminological work since the adoption of the Bertillon system and the finger-print identification."

"Well, you'll have to show me," said Dougherty, lighting a fresh cigar, sitting down and leaning back.

"Very well," said Thatcher Colt. He opened a door in the rear of the room and led in a goodlooking young man, slender and serious.

"Let me present Mr. Carl E. Leonard, one of the assistant state criminologists for Illinois. Mr. Leonard flew here in one of their departmental airplanes, at my personal request, just so that we could go through with this test. Vollmer recommended Mr. Leonard to me as an expert who could get the best results out of the machine. It does have a special technique of its own."

"I think it's childish," said Dougherty frankly. The young expert from Chicago only smiled and nodded his head as if he fully understood the District Attorney's skepticism. Thatcher Colt pressed a knob on the edge of the chair which registered its signal in some distant part of the house. By the time Colt had re-lighted his pipe, the door was opened and two uniformed men led in Doctor Maskell.

With the wraith of his familiar smile playing over his pale and haggard face, Doctor Maskell glanced at the table on which the lie detector lay exposed.

"Do you know what that machine is?" asked Thatcher Colt. Doctor Maskell's face expressed manifest contempt.

"Fake scientific apparatus," he jeered. "I've heard all about it. It is just about as scientific as the Abrams' blood detector machine. I can guess what it is by the looks of it."

Again the blonde young man smiled.

"It is not recognized in the New York Department," explained Thatcher Colt frankly. "So you do not have to submit to its use. Nor can you be bound in any way by any conclusions we may arrive at by its use. But it may break your story and give us clues by which we can finish our case against you."

"Yes, certainly," acquiesced Doctor Maskell, with magnificent indifference. I saw the look that passed between Dougherty and Thatcher Colt. Plainly the doctor's readiness only increased the District Attorney's suspicions. Doctor Maskell, in his opinion, like many another criminal, regarded himself as a superman. He was such an egoist that he felt confident that he could beat the machine.

It took very little time to adjust the apparatus to his chest and bared arm, as he sat in his shirt sleeves. Then Thatcher Colt began asking again the same questions with which Maskell had been battered for so long. They came, one after another, in a rattling fusillade, giving the suspect only time to answer before the next question was fired. For the first little while—certainly, for the first hour—the results would not be regarded as important. The unusual circumstances, the danger of Maskell's position, might easily make him nervous, and produce a jumpy chart, however innocent he might be. But Thatcher Colt knew that this state of preliminary fear would pass away. The subject of the lie detector is soon lulled into a sense of false security. As soon as he thinks he is giving a fine account of himself, he becomes more the master of his emotions. Then, and not until then, the records on the card become important indications. For an hour Colt talked to Maskell calmly about his journey—the same old story of giving out the Christmas presents, returning, and meeting the mysterious woman at his office door. But after that first hour, the tone, the pace, the very accent of the questions changed. The voice of Thatcher Colt became brittle, harsh, commanding, with an under-threat of malice in its tones. He stood, towering above the doctor, as if he held in his grasp the lightning of the electric chair. The very air of the room became tense and charged.

"What are you most afraid of in life, Doctor Maskell?"

"I am afraid of nothing."

"What are you most ashamed of in your life?" At this apparently simple question, we could almost hear the agitation of the electric pens, recording on the running ribbons of paper the heart and blood secrets of this erect and defiant man.

Both Dougherty and Thatcher Colt were studying the tape-like stream of paper emerging from the drum with the tell-tale graphs drawn upon them. Until this moment, the tracings had shown only debatable and indifferent variations, but a totally different result was obtained by the latest question. It had caused tremendous excitement within the dark spirit of this mysterious physician.

Up shot the graph of the heart line and with it leaped the diagram of the blood pressure. Why? Doctor Maskell hesitated and pondered his answer, while the Police Commissioner and the District Attorney waited in growing interest and astonishment.

"What are you most ashamed of in your life?" repeated Thatcher Colt. Experiment will prove that this question will bring to pause the busy thoughts of any human being, even if he is not accused of crime.

"Of nothing," declared Doctor Maskell, finally. But his voice was less confident than before and we knew from the lie detector that he was laboring under great excitement.

"Come, Doctor," urged Thatcher Colt patiently. "We are all ashamed of something."

"No."

"Are you ashamed of something in connection with the house on Peddler's Road?"

Again the extraordinary jiggle of emotions, traced by the electric pens on the moving tape, showed that the Commissioner had struck a sensitive vein in the doctor's emotional system.

"No," he repeated.

"Why did you keep that place on Peddler's Road?"

With every reference to the little portable cottage of blood and death the charts leaped at once into high peaks of emotional excitement and descended into valleys that might have recorded shame and despair.

"I like to have a place to hide away in."

"Alone?"

"Yes!"

Like stock brokers, Thatcher Colt and Dougherty were watching the tapes as they were fed into their hands by the silent young expert from Chicago. The District Attorney was exceedingly solemn and serious; he glanced at the

Commissioner as if to indicate that he was beginning to
have some respect for this apparatus.

"When were you last in the house on Peddler's Road?"

"About three weeks ago."

"Anyone with you then?"

"No."

"Had Geraldine Foster ever been there?"

"No."

"Are you certain?"

"I have no knowledge that she was ever there."

"But she was murdered there."

"I mean previously."

"Did you know she was going there this one time which
resulted in her death?"

"No."

The chart lines during these last few questions were
quite unimpressive. The emotional excitement in the
doctor seemed to pass away when Geraldine Foster was
brought into the question. No dizzy climbs of trace lines
appeared when the murder was mentioned. It was on some
subtler, obscurer point that he trembled. But who could
determine the meaning of this?

"Do you believe that murder is ever justified?"

"Yes."

"How do you mean that?"

"I have philosophical ideas on the subject. I believe in
euthanasia. But my notions have no bearing on this inquiry. I do not practice a philosophy opposed to the laws
under which I live."

"But doesn't your philosophy hold that murder is justified, even if it is opposed to the laws under which you
live?"

"Theoretically—yes."

"If sufficiently justifiable grounds arose, would you
commit murder in spite of the laws?"

"I don't know."

"Think again."

"I say, I don't know."

"Why did you quarrel with your brother George?"

"Because he did not approve of my private life."

"Did his wife also disapprove?"

"She did not know anything about it. What happened took place before she married my brother."

"Does she dislike you now."

"She does not know me. As I do not associate with my brother, I naturally do not know his wife. We have never met."

"Will you look at this?"

Thatcher Colt for the first time gave into Maskell's hands the note which George Maskell had written that morning. The physician was plainly astonished, no, delighted.

"That's the silver lining for all this," he remarked, with unsteady voice.

"There is nothing to indicate they don't know you," prodded Colt.

"No," said Maskell, smiling broadly. "No—that's what's so wonderful about it."

Certainly, if the lie detector machine was to be trusted, the doctor had been telling the truth during these last few questions. The lines ran in even, undulating curves like the waves of a peaceful sea.

"Your brother is a clever lawyer," resumed Colt, "but how do you intend to explain to him the lies you have been telling me."

"Lies?"

"Lies about your whereabouts on Christmas Eve. You know you have concealed the truth about that."

"I do not conceal the truth."

"You did not deliver those seven presents you told us about, while Checkles and the child were eating ice-cream. No one, doorman, footman, or elevator man, at the addresses you supplied, can remember your delivering those presents. Where were you?"

"I was where I said I was—delivering those presents!"

Until those last few exchanges, the chart had remained monotonous. But all passivity vanished when the doctor's whereabouts during the ice-cream episode was mentioned. There we had the high peaks again, an almost unmistakable accusation that Maskell was lying.

"You know that your insistence on this falsehood, which even this machine proclaims, subjects you to the gravest suspicions?"

"Unjustly so."

"Had you quarreled with Geraldine?"

"No—except about her marriage."

"Why, Doctor—are you sure?"

"Perfectly."

"She hadn't tried to obtain money from you?"

"Blackmail? Why, of course not."

"No?"

Thatcher Colt pulled the paper ribbon over far enough for the doctor to see it.

"Look at that graph and admit that you lied, Doctor Maskell. I am afraid you are your own worst enemy in this investigation, Doctor."

"You're showing yourself guilty as hell!" roared Dougherty.

Doctor Maskell shrugged his shoulders and lit a cigarette.

"What are your next questions?" he demanded. "I tell you that Geraldine Foster was above trying to blackmail anybody."

I could see, then, that Thatcher Colt had been holding back all this time the evidence of the blackmail note, rescued from the waste-paper. He was not giving his hand away. Not knowing it had been found, the physician would be unable to prepare a defense against it, and when the evidence was exploded at the trial it might easily seal his doom.

"Why do you suppose Geraldine Foster told Betty Canfield she wished she was dead and that she might soon be dead?"

"I don't know."

"Haven't you any suspicions?"

"No."

"You told us you were surprised about the bottle of tannic acid delivered to your office."

"I was."

"But you didn't call up the chemist and ask him to explain?"

"I beg your pardon—I did."

"He doesn't remember it."

"I talked to his clerk,—I think the young man is now away from the store with pneumonia."

This fact, Thatcher Colt subsequently checked and found correct. The clerk was delirious and could not be questioned.

"The clerk told me," continued Maskell, "that Geraldine called up and said I needed the stuff in a hurry, that was how it came. She ordered several bottles, three of which were left at my office."

Dougherty laughed.

"Pretty cool," he said. "Evidently you would like to make yourself appear the victim of a gigantic plot. Some mysterious enemy—perhaps, the dead girl herself—planting evidence against you, framing you—bah! It won't go down, Doctor."

All this time the graph was as calm as the waves of a summer sea. No sign of excitement in the doctor at all. Yet here, it seemed to me, he was being questioned on the most vital part of the case.

"Did Geraldine confide in you?"

"No."

"You don't know then, if she was having a secret affair with any one?"

"I do not. Nor do I believe it."

"Are you in need of money, Doctor?"

Again came that flashing smile, spontaneous, unforced and genuine.

"I am not," he answered firmly. "I have a small private fortune, and I am heir to one-half of my father's estate which will make me something like a millionaire."

Thatcher Colt hesitated for a moment. By the chart, flowing from the drum of the lie detector, it was evident that he was on a cold trail. He decided to try a new track.

"Have you any explanation for the extraordinary fact that Geraldine Foster's coat and purse were found in your office, days after the murder had been committed?"

"No, but I ask you, if you were a murderer, would you have left them there?"

Dougherty got mad at that defensive question. Rushing up to the doctor, he shook his finger admonishingly.

"It is not for you to argue your case," he snarled. "A clever murderer might have left the coat and purse there as proof of his innocence."

The doctor threw his cigarette into the fireplace and coolly lighted another. Outwardly, at least, he seemed as calm as if the examination were only just beginning.

"Have you formed any theory in your mind as to who that woman was—the woman whose face you never did see, and who came to your office door late in the afternoon of the murder?"

"No."

"Could it have been Betty Canfield?"

"No."

"You once told me it could not have been Geraldine?"

"According to your calculations, she was dead at the time?"

"Could it have been any of your patients?"

"I don't think so."

Simultaneously the chart rose and fell with palpitations of manifest concern.

"I repeat—could it have been one of your patients?"

"No," Maskell answered deliberately. But by the machine we knew again that the doctor was not being honest with us. Thatcher Colt put his hands on the doctor's shoulders.

"Suppose," he said, "that you were in love with a woman whose name you are protecting."

The tell-tale chart told us that the doctor was inwardly in emotional agitation.

"Suppose," went on Colt relentlessly, "that you and she hid yourselves away in the house on Peddler's Road."

Now the doctor's graph was maniacal in its weird convolutions.

"Suppose that Geraldine Foster had some hold on you. And you killed her to remove an obstacle. Would that be far from the truth, Doctor Maskell?"

The voice of the Commissioner was deadly.

"No," said Doctor Maskell. "No! No! I did not kill Geraldine Foster."

"Where are the dead girl's clothes?" demanded Thatcher Colt.

"I don't know. I did not kill her. I did not lift my hand against her."

"Had you any reason to?"

"No."

"Do you know that the refuse cleaned from under Geraldine's nails contained bits of small hair left after a recent barbering, and this afternoon I established that those hairs correspond to your own?"

There was a wriggle of lines on the chart, and the doctor gave a deep sigh that was like a lamentation.

Was not this a sign of weakening of the strong man's resistance? Believing it to be so, Dougherty sprang forward shouting:

"Why did the murderer use an axe, Doctor?"

"I don't know."

"Haven't you formed any theory as to the murder of that poor girl—hacking away her life with a double-bladed axe, filling the floors with blood, so that the very pigeons died—and laying her naked in that shallow grave?"

Here an extraordinary thing happened. The line of the heart and the blood pressure both remained at their normal fluctuations. They showed no trace of excitement. Thatcher Colt looked puzzled. But the District Attorney's voice was triumphant.

"Well, I'll tell you why an axe was used," he bellowed, with sudden fury. "You knew the story about Bruce Foster. You knew his father had killed a man with an axe and swung for it, down in Maryland. And you thought you could kill the girl and throw the crime on him."

A smile came into the face of Thatcher Colt and a gleam of amusement into his eyes.

"Bravo," he cried. "Dougherty, I wouldn't have given you credit for that. To think of axe murders running in a family!"

"Is that what happened, or isn't it?" shouted Dougherty. "You tell me, Doctor Maskell, if it isn't time for you to come through."

The doctor shrugged his shoulders and made no reply. Then Thatcher Colt interceded.

"I would like the doctor to leave the room for a minute," he said. "He needs a rest anyway."

The District Attorney looked astonished and confounded. Certain that he was on the point of driving the doctor into a corner, of getting a confession then and there, he stared at Thatcher Colt in red and choleric indignation.

"Listen to me," he began, but stopped, seeing the significant expression in Thatcher Colt's somber eyes. At a sign from Colt, the young man from the west removed the plates and tubes and covered up the lie detector machine. Two policemen came back and led the doctor off, and Leonard followed.

The moment we were alone, Dougherty exploded.

"Good God, Colt!" he cried. "You shouldn't have done that. We've clinched this case now. Maskell is guilty as red-fire hell."

But Thatcher Colt shook his head mysteriously.

"We are making progress," he conceded. "But we have still not reached our goal. We must turn to a new and more dangerous expedient. Have you ever heard of the truth drug?"

13

THE TRUTH DRUG

Dougherty ran his thick red hands through his mop of ruddy curls; his blue eyes rolled upward, and he swore.

"The truth drug!" he moaned. "More bunk. Are you out of your senses? We have got a case against that fellow now—one that will convince any twelve men you pick. The job is done, and the guy is just about ready to kick in. And then you—"

"Stop making speeches," said Thatcher Colt, with a glance of enjoyment up from the bowl of his pipe. "Suppose Maskell is innocent?"

"Innocent as Cain! Innocent as Landru! Innocent as Jack the Ripper!"

The District Attorney began marching up and down the room, talking to himself and checking off on his pudgy fingers the various points established against Doctor Maskell. Halting suddenly, he thrust forward his head and barked:

"What makes you think Maskell might be innocent?"

"This lie detector chart, for one thing."

"Why, if your chart proves anything at all, it proves his guilt!" howled Dougherty.

"No, it proves merely that he lied," corrected Thatcher Colt. "And look here—at the real mystery! The reactions of Doctor Maskell to questions about the murder itself were absolutely negative. See where we mentioned axe, blood, body, grave—everything gruesome you could think of—the chart remains perfectly normal."

"The fellow has himself in hand, that's all."

"But no—at other questions he has not himself in hand at all. Every reference to the house on Peddler's Road, for instance, makes him nervous."

"You caught him off his guard."

Thatcher Colt patiently shook his head and smiled.

"No, Dougherty. Observe that I went over the same ground not once but several times. Undoubtedly the doctor is hiding something from us—I don't think it would take a mind-reader to guess a part, at least, of what it is—a mysterious, unnamed lady, whose very existence the physician is prepared to deny. Suppose the doctor is innocent, but rather than involve her in the matter, the gallant doctor has lied. He is telling some most maladroit falsehoods, and has involved himself dangerously, yet he seems fatalistically determined to go to the electric chair, rather than snitch."

Dougherty sniggered and shook his head as if he considered the Police Commissioner a helpless case.

"The house was a place of rendezvous, all right—but there was no mystery about the lady. She was Geraldine Foster and when Maskell got tired of her, he chopped her up with an axe."

"But just suppose it was another woman—then what?"

"Why suppose it? Why should any man go to such preposterous lengths to shield any woman?"

Dougherty shrugged his shoulders and glanced at the watch on his wrist.

"It is eleven o'clock. I gave you my word that I would not act until midnight. Clearly Maskell is guilty as hell. Why not arrest him here and now?"

Thatcher Colt gravely shook his head. Out of a wall-closet he brought a small black bag, like that of a medical man. This bag he placed on the table where the lie detector machine had rested, then, by the buzzer in his chair he recalled the two policemen who presently led in to us again the still firm-jawed but considerably paler Doctor Humphrey Maskell.

Thatcher Colt rose suddenly from his chair and held out his hand.

"Doctor Maskell," he exclaimed, "if you are a murderer, you are a wonder. You have shown colossal nerve to submit to this examination."

The doctor smiled. Astute as he was, he did not realize the trick that was being played upon him. Criminals and honest men, too, like to be told they are bold and clever. Vanity is one of the greatest weaknesses of crook and saint alike.

"Is your nerve still good?" asked Thatcher Colt, with a trace of skepticism in his low voice.

"What is it now?" asked the doctor, the contempt again coming into his tone. "The trial by fire and water, like the ancient savages? Or divination by birds? Or what?"

"Have you ever heard of scopolamine?" asked Thatcher Colt.

"Yes. Erroneously called the 'truth serum' in the news-papers."

The doctor folded his hands and studied Thatcher Colt keenly.

"Why should I subject myself to a charlatan's drug when I don't have to?" he snapped. "As I understand it, you have no legal right to use the machine or the drug on me? I think I have been too acquiescent—now I am about fed up."

Thatcher Colt nodded.

"Correct," he admitted. "You are not compelled to do what I ask. Neither the lie detector nor the truth drug have ever been officially adopted by the Police Department of New York, although other cities, including Los Angeles, have officially adopted them."

"The truth drug?" The doctor's voice was incredulous, full of the scorn of the orthodox man of medicine. "A drug to make a man tell the truth—against interest, as the lawyers say. It must be a most remarkable concoction. Did you invent it?"

"Scopolamine," replied Thatcher Colt, "was first presented to the police by a physician and criminologist, Doctor R. E. House, of Ferris, Texas."

Doctor Maskell now wore the expression of a skeptical medical man facing an empiric; for the moment he forgot that he was a prisoner.

"What is the theory of this drug to which you want me to entrust my life?"

"The principle is very simple," returned Thatcher Colt. "You are aware that the most active and the most powerful of the five senses is the sense of hearing. This sense of hearing—with its supersensitivity and super-activity—is the last sense to be annihilated under the influence of an anesthetic. Also it is the first sense to be reawakened when the effect of the anesthetic wears off. Long after we cannot see or feel, taste or smell anything on the operation table, we can still hear—and we can still talk."

"True," nodded Doctor Maskell.

"If you have ever fainted, you may recall that before you opened your eyes you heard sounds, voices of people around you, or other disturbances. There is a period of time in which you hear, but are still not really conscious—a period when your ego has not yet asserted itself."

"Yes."

"Well, there is where scopolamine comes in. It lulls all the other senses to sleep except hearing. It is the theory of the inventor—and I may add, of myself—that during that period when you can hear, but cannot exercise your other senses, it is impossible, even for a clever man like yourself, to tell a lie."

"Humph!" said Doctor Maskell, enigmatically, with a strange look at Thatcher Colt. "This is a real challenge. You maintain that under the influence of this drug I could not exercise my will power to withhold the answer to any questions, if I so wished?"

"Exactly."

"And do these super-scientists who equip the police with these marvelous police devices have no fear that the instinct for self-preservation may not interfere with your pretty little medicine?"

"A large number of cases show that it does not," replied Thatcher Colt. "I could sit here and cite cases to you, but there isn't time. The stuttering young man of Meridian, Texas, was one example. There was also the case of O'Leary, known as the walking dead man."

Doctor Maskell smiled with a trace of malice.

"Do you think that District Attorney Dougherty would be convinced if I maintained my innocence under the influence of the drug?" he asked mockingly.

Thatcher Colt calmly re-lighted his pipe.

"The District Attorney wants the truth as much as you or I," he argued.

"I'll try anything once," declared Dougherty, his head to one side, as he closed one eye and looked at Maskell skeptically. Strange that both these men, each distrusting the other, equally distrusted the drug of truth. Suddenly Doctor Maskell came to a resolution. He stood up, took off his coat, rolled up his sleeves, and bared his large, heavily muscled arm, bristling with long, black hairs.

"Let's go," was all he said.

All the notes of what was said and done there, after
the needle was plunged into the doctor's arm and he was
stretched out on a couch in Thatcher Colt's library, now
lie before me. They are the most unusual I have ever taken
in any criminal case, for they show Doctor Maskell speaking without any reserve whatever. Stretched out there, he
was utterly relaxed. His eyes were closed. His breathing
was deep and regular. His voice was first heavy and deci-
sive and almost orotund in its importance, but gradually
it sank into a monotone, like the murmur of a sick person
talking in a fevered sleep.

"Doctor, did you kill Geraldine Foster?"

"I did not."

"Did you attack her with an axe?"

"I did not."

"Did you hate Geraldine Foster?"

"No."

"Did you love her?"

"No."

"Did you have any reason to kill Geraldine Foster?"

"Yes."

We all leaned forward toward the prostrate doctor as
he made that confession. The silence was intense, until
Thatcher Colt's brittle voice broke the silence.

"What reason did you have to kill her?"

"Because she threatened someone I love."

"To whom did she threaten to betray you?"

"To another woman."

"Who is this other woman?"

"My wife!"

We looked at each other in complete astonishment. I
suppose that I, too, am a sentimentalist. But in the face
of this amazing confession, I felt some kind of compassion
for the helplessness of this strong man, this giant who

possessed over himself such vast self-control, but who now lay like a fevered child, telling on himself. But if Thatcher Colt shared my feeling, he did not show any indications of it. Boldly he shot the next questions.

"Your wife! How long have you been married?"

"Fourteen years."

"When did you separate?"

"Ten years ago."

"You were not divorced?"

"No!"

The voice of the doctor had become very weary. "She will not give me a divorce. That was why I went away. To Reno. But I came back when—"

"When what?"

"When I saw that Geraldine was really missing and that it looked funny about me."

"What did Geraldine threaten?"

"To expose a beautiful love—drag it through the courts—and blacken the name of one I love."

"Who is that one?"

"I—won't—answer—that."

"How did Geraldine Foster know about your wife?"

"I don't know."

"Didn't you ask her?"

"No."

"Why?"

"I had no opportunity."

Then Thatcher Colt came back to that old sensitive spot in the doctor's mind.

"Why are you so stubborn about where you spent the time when Checkles and Doris were eating their ice-cream?"

"Because I will not drag her into it."

"Who?"

"I—won't—answer—that."

"Her name?"

"Again I say, I will not tell it."

Thatcher Colt gave Dougherty a swift glance, and the two men bent low over the powerful man who was now grumbling like a man in fever.

"Why were you with her?"

"I was not with her. I was waiting for her."

"Why?"

"Because it looked like an attempt had been made to trap us."

"Tell me."

"Mrs. Westock said that I was wanted at the house on Peddler's Road."

"Yes. Well?"

"It seemed strange to me. Because I knew the lady in the case, whom I very deeply adore and respect—do you understand that?"

His voice had become querulous, more than ever like the tones of a fevered patient. "Do you? I won't talk if you don't."

"Of course we understand that, Doctor, old boy," said Dougherty, in the soft tones of a deceiver.

"I didn't mean you," answered the doctor sleepily. "You don't matter to me. What does Mr. Colt say?"

As Dougherty retreated, scowling, Thatcher Colt said, in a voice full of eagerness and conviction:

"I fully understand that, Doctor. Please proceed."

"Well, I first went to the telephone and called up the lady as I had suspected she was at home. Fortunately, she was alone. I explained what had happened. She said she would come and meet me—and told me of a note she had from Geraldine, demanding blackmail."

"Where did you meet her?"

"We arranged to meet casually at an auction in an art gallery nearby. But she did not appear. Later I learned that circumstances made it impossible for her to leave the house."

"And you spent the next hour waiting for her in the art gallery?"

"I did—more than an hour."

"During that time, did any one see you who could testify to your presence there?"

Subsequently, when Colt had these statements checked, not one person could remember having seen Doctor Maskell in the auction room.

"I did my best to remain inconspicuous."

"In that time, you could have gone to Peddler's Road and committed the murder."

"I didn't do that."

"The lady will testify to these facts?"

"I will not permit her. I will not name her."

"She will come forward on her own account then?"

"Not if I can prevent it."

"You would rather die than involve her?"

"Undoubtedly."

"Why?"

"For a good reason."

"That is the sort of yarn that Chapman, the super-bandit tried to put over. Why don't you try to be original?" Dougherty fleered.

As Thatcher Colt gave the District Attorney an uneasy glance, he fell into a grinning, triumphant silence.

"Don't you realize, Doctor, that if there is such a lady, the police will find her?"

"I do not have any fear of that."

"Do you believe it was your wife who was laying that trap for you."

"Perhaps."

"Could she have killed Geraldine Foster and tried to put it on you?"

"She is cunning and cruel."

"Do you know this key?"

Thatcher Colt placed in the doctor's hands the key that had been found in the coat pocket of Geraldine Foster.

"Yes. It is the key to the house on Peddler's Road."

"How did Geraldine get hold of it."

"I don't know."

"Why was the pillow case put over her head?"

"I don't know."

"Was the pillow case the property of the lady you are protecting?"

"I don't know."

"You saw the pillow case?"

"Yes."

"Did you buy that pillow case?"

"I don't know anything about pillow cases."

"What is your wife's full name and where does she live?"

There was no answer. Thatcher Colt bent over the huge form, listless and sprawling in the chair.

At the same moment, there came a hasty rapping on the door. As Thatcher Colt seemed more concerned about the unreplying doctor, I went to the door. As I opened it, Hogan burst past me with the furious force of a football player. He was panting with haste and excitement and held in front of him a bulky bag-like object.

"Hogan!" cried Dougherty, "What's up?"

Instead of replying, Hogan cast his bundle on the floor. It was a pillow case embroidered with rosebuds—a duplicate of the one found over the head of Geraldine Foster. No one spoke as Hogan dramatically removed the contents and held them up, piece by piece, for inspection.

They were the blood-stained clothes of the murdered girl.

"Where did you get these?" asked Colt crisply.

"I found them in a closet in the office of Doctor Maskell," gasped Hogan, with a grin at the prone figure on the couch.

"Now we'll talk turkey!" exploded Dougherty.

But Thatcher Colt, even then, tried to stay the determination of the District Attorney.

"Doctor Maskell has fallen asleep," he protested.

"To hell with that," answered Dougherty. "This man killed Geraldine Foster. Wake up, Maskell."

The District Attorney seized the sleeping doctor and shook him roughly. Blearily, the prisoner opened his eyes and peered up at his captor, who drew a document from his pocket.

"Doctor Maskell," he said, "I arrest you under a short affidavit, charging you with the murder of Geraldine Foster. Here is the warrant!"

The doctor managed a feeble smile, closed his eyes and fell instantly back into slumber.

At a signal from the Commissioner, the two police attendants carried the unconscious prisoner out of the library. Then Thatcher Colt faced Merle Dougherty.

"Going through with this farce?" he asked.

"Farce?"

"Yes. You think this was a crime of passion. It was not. It was a cold-blooded, business proposition—and I do not believe that the murderer and victim were even acquainted with each other."

"Colt, sometimes I think you are mad."

"Mad, because I do not believe Maskell is guilty?"

"He will be indicted tomorrow and burn before Thanksgiving," predicted Dougherty, rising on his toes and lifting his eyebrows.

"Attaboy!" crowed Hogan, putting the clothes back into the pillow case. As a County Detective, Hogan could say this. If he had belonged to the Police Department, Colt would have put him on a beat where he could chase goats in the Bronx for his impertinence.

"For heaven sake, listen to reason, Dougherty. Maskell is as innocent of this crime as you are. And if you give me time, I'll prove it and deliver the guilty person into your hands."

Dougherty put his hands on his hips.

"Colt," he remonstrated, "you're impossible. I have been more patient with you than any man in my position should be. But now I'm through. Maskell killed Geraldine Foster and he's going to fry for it."

"And what if later I prove you wrong?"

"I'll be the first to apologize."

"But suppose Doctor Maskell has been electrocuted by that time?"

The District Attorney shook his head sadly.

"He'll be electrocuted a long, long time before you or anybody else proves him innocent," he retorted confidently. "You're through with this case now. Forget it. Hogan will clear up the details for me and we'll rush the case to trial—I'll be ready in three weeks."

Thatcher Colt folded his arms, and said quietly: "Nevertheless, the police department will go on with the work—it does not regard this case as closed."

They were friends, but no one could have guessed it to see them regarding each other there like antagonists preparing for a struggle.

"You will keep your ideas to yourself, unless you can prove them?" asked Dougherty uneasily.

"Absolutely—until I am ready. Will you have another glass of port, Dougherty?"

"Don't care if I do," said the District Attorney heartily.

And the two men, in spite of the tension of the moment before, were still able to clink glasses and drink. But

I kept my eye on my chief and I was not surprised when he let fly a handful of parting arrows.

"Dougherty," he said, "before you can convince me of the guilt of Doctor Maskell, there are four questions you will have to answer."

"And they are?"

"Why was Geraldine Foster killed with an axe? Would it not have been simpler to shoot her, poison her—instead of all that blood-letting?

"Why was she stripped nude, *after* the murder?

"Why was the pillow case over her head?

"Who was the mysterious woman the doctor found at the door?"

Dougherty laughed as he shook hands with Thatcher Colt.

"Come to the trial," he shouted, "and you'll hear the answer to all your questions."

14
THATCHER COLT'S SECRET

The midnight arrest of Doctor Humphrey Maskell, made in the home of the Police Commissioner, naturally set the papers frenzied with excitement. New York could talk of nothing else.

Unmoved by George Maskell's open denunciation of the methods of the District Attorney, Dougherty went straight ahead with his purpose. Early the next morning he appeared before the Grand Jury, bringing with him a parade of witnesses. On our way to lunch, Thatcher Colt and I passed by the closed door of the Grand Jury room and my chief nudged me and said in a low voice:

"Observe the two old men lounging at opposite sides of the door?"

I looked and instantly recognized one of the elderly watchers as Edmund L. Foster, the father of the murdered girl. But who was the other—the short, infinitely neat and feeble old gentleman with the gloved slim hands, the walking stick and the gardenia in his buttonhole?

"That is old Alexander Maskell, the millionaire architect," exclaimed my chief. "Thus the father of the victim and the father of the accused face each other at the Grand Jury's door. Nice touch for the tabloids tomorrow."

But the expression on the face of Thatcher Colt was not amused. It seldom was when he passed the Grand Jury

room. As we hastened to our favorite lunch room, he talked vigorously of his disagreement with the District Attorney and his case against Maskell.

"But think of the evidence—" I ventured.

"The Grand Jury will eat it up. That is what is the trouble with our Grand Jury system. There you have a bunch
of men, twenty-three of them, with sixteen constituting a
quorum, and if only twelve of those men think that Maskell is guilty, they will vote a true bill, find an indictment,
and leave a stain on his character for the rest of his life.
All this, and remember, Tony, that only one side will be
heard by those Grand Jurors. Almost always, Dougherty,
or any other District Attorney, can get the indictment he
wants. I know, and you know, that an indictment is not
supposed to count against a man's character. But it does,
just the same. The general public always believes the indicted man guilty and if he eventually is discharged, they
generally think it was due to some kind of influence. Even
if Maskell gets out of this, the indictment will ruin him.
The whole system is wrong, it is expensive and inefficient.
The Grand Jury acts upon a superficial knowledge of facts
and very little knowledge of the law. And so, I am ashamed
to say, in this particular case, does my old friend, Merle
Dougherty. He is making an ass of himself, and a martyr
out of Maskell."

Just as Colt had predicted, within a few hours the
Grand Jury had handed down the following indictment:

"THE PEOPLE OF THE
STATE OF NEW YORK
against
HUMPHREY MASKELL, M.D.
"The Grand Jury of the County of New York,
by this indictment, accuse Humphrey Maskell

of the crime of murder in the first degree, committed as follows:

"The said Humphrey Maskell, of the Borough of Manhattan, in the City of New York, in the County of New York aforesaid, on the twenty-fourth day of December last, at the borough and county aforesaid, in and upon one Geraldine Foster, with force of arms, commonly called an axe of double blade, wilfully and feloniously, with malice aforethought and with deliberate and premeditated design to effect the death of her, the said Geraldine Foster, he did, then and there, with the said axe, mortally wound her, the said Geraldine Foster, and inflict upon the body and person of her, the said Geraldine Foster, to wit: upon or through the head and brains, the stomach, the lungs, liver, face and jaw, wounds and injuries, from which wounds and injuries she, the said Geraldine Foster, died on the day aforesaid, at the town and county aforesaid, and that the death of her, the said Geraldine Foster, was caused and produced by the aforesaid wounds and injuries inflicted as aforesaid, and that the aforesaid wounds and injuries were inflicted as aforesaid by the said Humphrey Maskell, with force and arms, wilfully, and of malice aforethought, and with the deliberate and premeditated design of him, the said Humphrey Maskell, to effect the death of her, the said Geraldine Foster, and in manner and form aforesaid, and by means aforesaid he, the said Humphrey Maskell, did slay and kill her, the said Geraldine

Foster, against the form of the statute in such case made and provided and against the peace of the People of the State of New York and their dignity.

Merle Dougherty,
District Attorney."

Promptly, in accordance with the law, the prisoner was taken to the Homicide Court, presided over that morning by Municipal Magistrate Pearson. There, with great dignity and assurance, and in the face of a crowd of unfriendly spectators who made faces at him and cursed him—it seemed the whole town was already convinced of his guilt—the "smiling doctor of Washington Square" pleaded not guilty to the indictment and waived examination. With that formality, Doctor Humphrey Maskell passed completely out of the jurisdiction of the police, being taken over officially by the Department of Corrections, who put him into a cell in the City Prison which is called the Tombs.

During his brief examination before Magistrate Pearson, with his brother and sister-in-law standing by his side, I saw the doctor's gaze roving over the crowd in the court room, as if searching in vain for some well-beloved face. For whom was it he was looking, I wondered. Was it for a woman whose name he had refused to give, even when under the influence of the truth drug? Or was there no such person,—except the slain Geraldine. I had no idea, then, how close we were to the answer.

The secret activities in the office of Thatcher Colt, during the busy and exciting days that followed, are probably without parallel in the history of police procedure.

So far as the public was concerned, Colt had solved the murder of Geraldine Foster. Yet secretly, the Police Commissioner of New York City now set to work, bending all the energies of his department to undermine the very case he had presented to the District Attorney, to destroy what he believed to be the false case he had built up, and to find, instead, the really guilty person.

Meanwhile, the police and the District Attorney, the Grand Jury, and every one connected with the case were being complimented by the newspapers. Everybody seemed to expect the conviction of Doctor Maskell—by the man in the street he had already been condemned to the electric chair.

After reading an interview which Dougherty had given the papers, the Commissioner laughed softly and said to me:

"It is amazing what a convincing case Dougherty had in his hands. But he explains only one of the cardinal mysteries that I saw in the affair from the beginning—and I am convinced that his explanation is not the correct one. Why was an axe used? Because, says the District Attorney, Maskell wanted to throw suspicion on Bruce Foster, whose father was hung for an axe murder. If Geraldine dies, Bruce gets twice as much inheritance—so Maskell is supposed to have found even a motive for the man he meant to be suspected. If Maskell figured all that out, and tried to involve Bruce Foster he was a thirty-third-degree blunderer. On the other hand, why does not Dougherty just as well suppose that Bruce Foster really did it and planted evidence to convict the doctor?"

Every detail was hungrily reported by the newspapers and photographs filled the papers—pictures of Doctor Maskell in the Criminal Identification Bureau, being photographed, front view and profile, having his fingers inked and his impression recorded and his weight and height measured, of Doctor Maskell in the line-up, under the nine lamps above the platform in the old gymnasium at Police Headquarters, with hundreds of detectives

looking on while Mulrooney—then only a deputy inspector—barked out his questions. More, the papers recounted
gleefully the exotic foods for which the doctor expressed
a preference. On his second day at the Tombs, he ordered
green turtle steak, cooked in the Spanish fashion, brought
from a Sevillian restaurant on Pearl Street, where they
knew just how long to cook the steak.

The doctor was also photographed smiling from behind the bars of his cell, grinning defiance at Dougherty
who was pressing for an early trial, and capitalizing to the
full on his prosecution of a rich man's son. Dougherty was
an honest civil servant, but he was by no means blind to
opportunities for spectacular public impression. Of course,
the tabloids also sent their glibbest sob sisters to write up
the doctor. And soon after their stories appeared, the "mash
notes" began to arrive at the Tombs. Shop girls and brokers'
widows alike wrote to Doctor Maskell. Generally what they
told him was that they were sure he was innocent and would
help in any way they could, that all they needed was human
understanding which they had never known in their lives,
and so, they imagined, neither had he, and while the whole
world was against Doctor Maskell, they, the writers of these
notes, were absolutely for him—against the whole world.
Literally hundreds were for him in just that fashion.

Meanwhile, in Walter Winchell's column it was stated
that Betty Canfield, the roommate of the murdered Geraldine Foster, and Anthony Abbot, secretary to the Police
Commissioner, were "Garbo-Gilberting" which slang of
the moment, taken from the names of two romantic cinema players, meant that we were in love with each other.
Betty issued a stern denial, which Winchell declined to
print, upon which she wrote me a note, informing me that
she would never, never, never, never marry.

The prisoner made very few statements, but once gave
an interview that was widely discussed.

"I am proud," said he, "of the way my family is rallying to my support. My father told me here this morning, with this steel door between us, that I was the apple of his eye. Funny, but Mr. Thatcher Colt could not break me—he knows he could not break me with all the ingenuity of his third degree—but I did find tears in my eyes when my father said that to me. And brother George has undertaken my defense."

That was news, and as we expected, the papers played it up to the fullest advantage. There were pictures of the two brothers, taken with their arms over the shoulders of each other, in the cell at the Tombs.

The night that picture appeared, Thatcher Colt and I worked late in his office. Toward midnight, he shoved aside his papers and said:

"The Foster case, in spite of the fact that Dougherty believes Maskell will probably be electrocuted, as it stands, is anybody's puzzle. A number of people could have done it. But when I eliminate some of the clues tomorrow the range of choice will have narrowed down greatly. Then we shall see. After that there are some other essential clues which we are still lacking—some kick-shaws that seem to have no value—nameless, fantastic trifles which yet contain the vital and damning evidence that we really want."

For a moment he drew thoughtfully on his pipe.

"But Dougherty has muddied the waters and made them turbid," he complained. "There is still the mystery about why that crime was committed with an axe. There is still the question of who that mysterious woman was at the doctor's door."

"Do you believe in her?" I asked.

"I do. I know Doctor Maskell has been lying, but not about that. Ah, Tony, what mysteries are here. When was the girl's body buried? I wish I knew that. Why did they bother to bury it at all? I have found a witness, a passing motorist, who remembers seeing lights on the hill on the night of January 3—that probably was the night the strange burial was performed."

He glanced around him with the lightning eye of some predatory bird.

"We have two means of attack," he continued. "One is to eliminate the suspects."

"Let me name them," I said. "There is first the doctor himself."

"Yes."

"And after him Bruce and then Armstrong—who still can't account for his movements—and even the father had a motive, as you once pointed out—"

"Who else?" asked Thatcher Colt, with a tantalizing smile.

I scratched my head vainly.

"Ah, Tony," said my chief, "you have left out some of the most important suspects. But no matter, whether you named them or not, they are all innocent."

"All?"

"Every last one of them—as innocent as if Geraldine Foster were living this minute."

"How can you know that?" I insisted, for it did seem to me now that there was arrogance in the manner of Thatcher Colt.

"How?" he repeated, with a chuckle. "Well, Tony, I will tell you how."

Irritatingly he paused to light his pipe and then lifting his eyes, he stared at me somberly through the plumes of violet vapor.

"Because," he disclosed, "I have been certain from the first, that not only was another woman involved, but that Geraldine Foster was killed by a woman!"

15

THE PILLOW CASE CLUE

As if he fully sensed the cold chill that ran through me when he divulged his terrible suspicion, Thatcher Colt gazed at me with melancholy eyes.

"The clue," he said, "lies in this."

From a drawer in his desk he removed and spread before him the embroidered pillow case which we had found over the head of Geraldine Foster.

"I believe a woman did this crime," repeated Thatcher Colt. "You and I and the guilty creature herself are the only persons living who know that, Tony. And I have to find that woman by means of this pillow case."

"Didn't I gather there was no laundry mark?" Thatcher Colt nodded.

"It had never been to a laundry—it was new, but I shall find the owner without the laundry mark."

I looked at him incredulously. That seemed an utterly impossible feat.

"Come with me," he said, and leading the way, he marched into a small room, where there were about thirty detectives assembled. On a table lay a large pair of shears. As the detectives saluted, Thatcher Colt spread out the pillow case which he had carried in with him, cut it into thirty segments and gave one piece to each man.

Then in a brief speech to the stolid detectives, he recalled to them another famous case in which a pillow case
had led to the final solution of an apparently baffling
murder mystery. In some detail he told them of the work
done by Inspector Faurot in the slaying of Anna Aumüller,
whose torso was found floating in the river. Her head was
never found, but her murderer died for his crime, tracked
solely by a pillow case.

"If our criminals plagiarize from the past," remarked
Thatcher Colt, "why not our detectives?"

In both the Anna Aumüller case and the Geraldine Foster mystery, the pillow case was unusual and expensive.
The slip was of fine texture and should have come from
a shop that dealt in the finest quality of linens. Yet the
pillow case for all its fine quality, was a gaudy affair with
rosebuds embroidered on it.

Thatcher Colt then told his thirty detectives what he
wished them to do. He was talking to men distinguished
not for their imagination, their education, or their in-
telligence. Instead, they were known, like bull-dogs, for
getting their teeth into something and refusing to let go.
This job to which he assigned them was a hewing-of-wood
task, a drawing-of-water duty, but such work is vital, and
it is of supreme consequence to the police detection of
crime, as the results in this case showed. Not one of the
detectives was told that they were working on the Geraldine Foster case. Each of them was assigned by Thatcher
Colt to a section of the city in which were located the lofts
and sample rooms of manufacturers and agents known to
deal in bedding and bed linen. Off they went, each with
his own sample.

All day long, day in and day out, for the next three
days, these detectives travelled from building to building,
visiting every office, questioning every maker and distrib-
utor of pillow slips, exhibiting the samples in an organized

effort to track this unmated pillow case to its source. I will admit that it seemed like a sheer waste of man power, nor could I guess even its purpose. What could be proved, even if they did locate the wholesaler from which it came? But Thatcher Colt has a profound regard for facts. He feels that the more facts you know about anything, the nearer you are likely to come to the truth about it. On this principle, he continued his men on this most depressing chase, depressing because visit after visit yielded not the slightest result. Each night the thirty men reported to Thatcher Colt at Police Headquarters in deep dejection.

But my chief refused to be discouraged.

"If we don't find some jobber in New York who recognizes this pillow case," he declared, "we'll visit every mill in the country before I will quit."

Each manufacturer or agent when shown a sample shook his head and declared that it was not in his line. In this, which the others found so discouraging, Thatcher Colt found comfort.

"When they are able to state so positively, and at once, that it is not theirs, that makes our work all the easier," he declared. "It would really look hopeless if they said they were not sure."

At the beginning, Colt was an ignoramus about pillow cases, but before he got through he knew a great deal about them. His tenacity, in view of repeated failures, seems all the more remarkable to me as I look back on it.

It was Detective Sergeant Gernsback, a stolid, reliable fellow, who finally came proudly to the Commissioner's office with tidings. Gernsback had taken his piece of the pillow into the office of a manufacturer's agent who promptly identified it as part of his own line.

"Ah, yes," he had told the detective. "I remember it very well. I have good cause to. It cost me a lot of money."

He had then explained to Gernsback that these expensive pillow cases, of which the piece shown to him was undoubtedly a sample, had been sold by his house to a number of small stores scattered throughout New York City. The pillow cases had been made up in the nature of an experiment. Despite their excellent quality, their gaudiness had made them almost unsalable. The people who could afford that quality wouldn't stand for that style, and the people who liked the style, invariably could not afford the quality. Thus the manufacturers were left with almost the entire output unsold on their hands. For years they had been carried in stock, because of hopes which never materialized, and finally to prevent a total loss, had been offered at a great sacrifice to a lot of little junky stores throughout Manhattan.

"Has he got the sales slips?" asked Thatcher Colt.

Well, as to that, Detective Gernsback couldn't say. The Commissioner hadn't ordered him to find out anything about sales slips. What he had asked him to do was to find the origin of the pillow cases and that, Detective Gernsback, who seemed to think his good fortune was an evidence of superior cunning and competence, had triumphantly accomplished. Sales slips were no part of his thoughts and by voice and rolling eyes he gave the Commissioner to understand that.

"Come on, Tony," said Thatcher Colt, "let's go down there and see what we can find."

The office of the Wigglestaff Pillow and Case Factory was just off Fifth Avenue in the Thirties—a crowded region, with dark buildings brass-plated with foreign names and trundle wagons dodging through the trucks and limousines, pushed by men whose faces were hidden by the racks of dresses and coats which they propelled. Mr. Pearlman, the Manhattan agent for the Wigglestaff Company, was greatly flattered when Thatcher Colt entered his office, and his three stenographers stared up open-mouthed from their machines at the immaculate Police Commissioner.

With suave kindness, Thatcher Colt explained what we were there for. Did Mr. Pearlman keep records of all his sales? Mr. Pearlman hemmed and hawed and said well, yes and no, and he couldn't be sure without looking. These particular pillow cases had been sold for cash and the duplicate delivery slips might have been destroyed. However, if we didn't mind waiting, he would investigate.

Presently he returned with the duplicate delivery slips in his hand. For this time, at least, we were playing in luck—that element which Thatcher Colt maintains cannot be disregarded in the investigation of a crime, the conduct of a war, or any other gamble in human affairs. As he gave the slips into the Commissioner's hands, Mr. Pearlman explained that every one of the pillows and cases was accounted for by those little pieces of paper.

Seven stores had bought those cases. I quickly made stenographic notes of the names and addresses, and cutting short the effusive conversation of Mr. Pearlman, who would have a great story to tell his undoubtedly large family at the dinner table that night, we hurried off, Thatcher Colt, Gernsback and I, to make the round of the shops.

They were in widely separated areas. Again we were in an automobile—Neil McMahon was at the wheel, driving first to a little dry-goods and notions shop on Third Avenue. The proprietor was a loud-voiced, heaving and asthmatic Irish woman, who was not impressed at all by the three of us, but immediately on hearing our questions called down a pox of boils on the maker of those pillow cases. She had bought them at a bargain and yet had never been able to sell one pair of them. They were still on her shelves. We counted them up, checking them against the quantity indicated on the delivery sheet and found that her indignation was justified. . . . She still had them all.

Again we sallied forth, and again luck favored Thatcher Colt. We found ourselves at the store of one Joseph Schnutz, a dealer in household furnishings, in Fourteenth Street, and to Thatcher Colt's delight he learned at once that Mr. Schnutz was a man of accounts and entries, a careful merchant who had exhaustive records of all his transactions.

"Did you buy any pillow cases like this one?" asked Thatcher Colt, thrusting the piece which Gernsback had used, under his eyes.

Indeed he had, Mr. Schnutz fervently declared that he considered those pillow cases the most beautiful he had ever handled in his thirty-five years as a merchant in this neighborhood.

"Did you ever sell any of them?" asked Thatcher Colt.

Mr. Schnutz sadly shook his head.

"Only one pair," he replied. "The people of today are altogether lacking in an artistic appreciation of beautiful things."

But did he know to whom he had sold them?

"I remember the sale perfectly," said the merchant to Thatcher Colt. "It was a lady with a little girl—pretty little girl—who bought that pair of pillow cases, after she saw them in the window. Where is that sales check?"

With folded arms and an expression of the deepest melancholy, Thatcher Colt waited. He did not seem in the slightest degree disconcerted when the merchant, having found the paper he sought, put his glasses on the tip of his nose and calmly read from one of his sales slips:

"The name was Mrs. Felise Morgan, of 186 Washington Square, North."

The pillow slip which was found over the head of the buried Geraldine Foster had been purchased by the mother of little Doris Morgan.

16
THE MYSTERIOUS LADY

At once I became a prey to the most hideous and fantastic suspicions.

First it seemed to me as if this latest discovery completely shattered all possibility of Doctor Maskell's innocence. In another instant my rapid-changing theories would clear the physician, only to conjure before me an entirely different and unthinkable accusation.

Had Felise Morgan killed Geraldine Foster?

Even at this late date, when so many of the clues were already obviously at hand, even after what Thatcher Colt had said to me, I rejected the idea as impossible. A woman wield that murderous axe, deal those awful blows, and then, alone and unaided, bury that body after soaking it in a bathtub full of tannic acid? I felt like shuddering at the very notion.

Why should Felise Morgan want to kill Geraldine? Unless it was because she was in love with Doctor Maskell and was jealous or afraid. The mother of little Doris must be the woman whose name the physician had kept so loyally.

I glanced at Thatcher Colt, beside whom I sat in the department car. He was watching me with an amused and almost paternal smile.

"It's hard to figure out, isn't it?" he said banteringly. "But one thing now is perfectly clear."

"What is that?"

"Doctor Maskell is in love with Felise Morgan."

"You think that a woman as lovely—"

"I put nothing beyond the possibilities. God knows that women have killed women before, and they have not scrupled to use an axe, if it suited their purposes."

"Is that why, do you think, Doctor Maskell is so secretive about it?"

"Did you notice the love beaming in his eye when he looked at Doris, the day we rode around town in the car?"

"I did observe that."

"For that child he would do anything. It is a case of mad heroics, I suppose. Maskell would rather take all the blame even if innocent than ruin the life of that little girl. He may even think Felise is guilty. He possibly remembers Ruth Snyder and her child."

"Do you actually think Mrs. Morgan is guilty?"

Thatcher Colt shook his head in plain perplexity.

"That is what I have come here to find out," he replied.

We were at the north side of Washington Square, once more in front of the house in which Doctor Maskell had his offices, and on the second floor of which lived Doris Morgan and her beautiful mother.

As we started up the stairs, a man passed us, coming out. He was a thick-set, heavy shouldered man, wrapped in a large fur overcoat, and he hurried down the street with a swaggering, self-conscious gait. As he passed us, he gave us one disdainful glance. The next moment, some one else ran down the steps, chattering in a low voice to himself. It was Checkles, the doctor's hunch-backed chauffeur, and he was plainly bent on following the first man.

"Just seeing where he goes—I suspect him," cried Checkles to Thatcher Colt, as he leaped to the sidewalk and hopped away.

"Who on earth is the man Checkles is following?" I asked.

"That is Gilbert Morgan—the father of Doris, and the husband of Felise."

I was tingling with suspense as we approached the door of the Morgan apartment, the same door before which we had stood the night we had first visited Betty's apartment. After ringing, we had barely time to catch our breath before the door was opened by a tall, long-armed woman with severe features and thin black hair brushed tightly over her head. She looked at us with cyes that seemed to burn their way past all our barriers of caution. She recognized Colt at once; he had been here before.

"Mrs. Morgan will see you in a moment," she said. "Please come in."

She led us down a wide hall, charmingly laid out and decorated, into a small cabinet-like place that opened off the grand drawing-room of the suite. Here we were left, to study the charming water colors on the wall, especially one aquarelle of a painted sail, which, as I learned later, had been done by Felise—she was an amateur painter. I looked at Thatcher Colt and was about to speak, when a scraping foot-step made me turn. To my astonishment, I saw an old woman creeping into the room. For all her extreme age and feeble condition, she was looking from my face to Thatcher Colt with eager and intelligent curiosity.

"Don't tell her I came in here, will you?" the old woman croaked, in a deep whisper.

We both promised, wonderingly. She came nearer to Thatcher Colt, choosing him by that unfailing instinct for authority that belongs to the very old and the very young. With her palsied fingers on his wrist, she said:

"Make Felise tell you the truth. She stays here because of me. I am not worth it. Tell her to follow her heart—I can take care of myself."

"Who are you?" asked Thatcher Colt.

"Her mother-in-law."

The old woman retreated to the door and then, looking over her left shoulder at the Commissioner, she added:

"You tell her that and make her do it and you may prevent another murder!"

With this cryptic utterance, she started out of the room. The tall, dark-eyed, hard-featured woman who had admitted us returned hurriedly and seemed to whisk the old woman bodily from our sight. As I turned and looked my astonishment at Thatcher Colt, he put his finger to his mouth, and walked across to another water-color, admiring it in low tones.

It was only a few minutes later that Felise Morgan entered the room.

The mistress of the apartment looked even more beautiful than when I had seen her, wrapped in furs, in the Police Commissioner's car. Now I saw that she was tall and slender, her figure exquisitely proportioned, and her coils of dark-red hair were wound around a pale and fragile face, characterized by refinement, taste and delicacy. The graceful curve of her scimitar brows arched above dark-green eyes of lustrous and almost chatoyant vitality and eagerness. As she approached us, coming from the drawing-room, she looked ethereal and lovely in a soft lavender negligee, her two hands clasped at her throat, and her eyes already studying us, as if sensing already that we were antagonistic, here to pry into the most secret chapters of her life.

The Police Commissioner rose and bowed profoundly.

"Mrs. Morgan," he said, "I came here on a most unpleasant duty."

"So the police have found out about Humphrey and me at last," she said with a sigh. Sinking into a small, wooden chair, she added: "I intended going to you. I could have saved you the trouble of tracing me. I was resolved to do so, no matter what the cost."

A smile, implying some kind of unspoken satisfaction, flitted across the mouth of Thatcher Colt.

"Hasn't the doctor forbidden you to speak?" he inquired.

"Who told you that?"

Thatcher Colt held up a protesting hand.

"Don't be under any misapprehensions," he said. "Doctor Maskell does not know I am here. He has no idea even that his relation to you is discovered. Only by keeping that fact quiet have I any hope of saving him."

"Saving him?" echoed Felise Morgan, slowly rising. "Why, you are the man who wants to kill him."

Thatcher Colt looked at her frankly.

"I am the man who gathered all the evidence on which the indictment was brought," he corrected. "But I have never believed him guilty. The District Attorney took the matter out of my hands and has gone ahead on his own course. Since the indictment, I have been seeking you. I want to arrest the *right* person."

She closed her eyes, and I could see that she was making a strong effort not to give way to her feelings.

"Why did you not go to Doctor Maskell about this?" she asked.

"He wouldn't trust me. Besides, I would give my hand away. Have we much time to talk?"

"I am afraid not. My husband—"

"Very well, then, I shall be quick. Did you or did you not receive a letter from Geraldine Foster shortly before she died?"

The pallor that suddenly swept across the beautiful face was a distressing thing to see. Stark terror came bounding to her eyes, looking out like a maddened and imprisoned animal. Thatcher Colt did not wait for her to answer.

"It demanded blackmail?"

"Yes."

"Have you the letter?"

"No—I destroyed it."

"Did you tell the doctor?"

"Yes."

"What did he say?"

"He was very, very angry."

"And ever since then, Mrs. Morgan, you have been afraid. And when her body was found, you believed—"

"No! No! I didn't believe it. I don't believe it now. Doctor Maskell was not capable of such a crime."

Thatcher Colt nodded.

"I believe you," he said. "Now, on the afternoon of Christmas Eve, did the doctor telephone you?"

"Yes. He said he had a message, apparently from me, to meet me at the house on Peddler's Road. He telephoned here to confirm it. I told him about the letter. We both saw at once there was something wrong, and I promised to meet him at once at an art gallery—Wilkinson's—nearby. But I was prevented from leaving the house."

"Prevented—by what?"

"By my husband," she answered, looking at the Commissioner with level gaze.

"You never did see Doctor Maskell in the Wilkinson Galleries, then—all that afternoon?"

"No."

"Didn't you get in touch with him at all?"

"No."

"Didn't you fear he would worry?"

"No. It often happens that I am prevented from leaving the house. The doctor understands about that."

Thatcher Colt stood up and took a hurried turn around the room. I noticed that this hurried walk carried him past two doors of the room in which we sat, and that he observed them closely. Then he came closer to Felise Morgan and bending over her, asked in a low voice:

"You are sincerely in love with Maskell?"

"I am."

"Would you divorce your husband and marry the doctor if you could?"

"Gladly."

"Why haven't you done it, then?"

With a gasp, Felise Morgan stood up, her eyes tragic.

"You don't know all, then?"

"No, indeed, I do not."

"The doctor went to Reno—"

"I knew that."

"We had both planned to go. He was to make arrangements. I was to follow with my little girl and also—"

Felise paused.

"I know," said Thatcher Colt, "that your husband has been a drug-fiend for years. I know the difficulties on both sides that you and Maskell have faced. I can understand your secret meeting place on Peddler's Road. But why have you waited so long?"

"It takes time to make up the mind in cases like this."

"Right! Now tell me—whom else did you mean to take with you?"

"His mother," she murmured. "A poor old woman with no one—"

She got no further but halted, all her body trembling. We heard the sound of a key turning in the lock, and heavy footfalls after the slam of the door. Down the hall-way strode the man that Thatcher Colt had pointed out to me in the street, the one Checkles had followed. At nearer view, and with his hat off, I saw what an unprepossessing fellow was this Gilbert Morgan. He was spherical and plump, with jowls that hung down in ruddy keeches of flesh. His shiny bald head was like a cupola, a hemispherical roof over his head. Through his pudgy, little black eyes, he looked at us malevolently.

"Felise, who are these men?" he asked in unctuous tones.

She hesitated, but before she could speak, Thatcher Colt had interceded.

"I am Thatcher Colt, the Police Commissioner of the City of New York," he suavely explained.

Was it fear that leaped in a scarlet dash across the face of the fat little man with the bald head? Or was it suspicion?

"The Police Commissioner?" he repeated, moistening his lips. "To what—"

"I shall tell you," interrupted Colt, with a debonair smile. "It is a very difficult matter. The police have received complaints against this apartment. Of screams, high quarrels—"

"Preposterous!" grated the husband of Felise Morgan.

"I felt so," agreed Thatcher Colt. "I know perfectly well a man of your position would not make scenes, or create disturbances. However, I could not ignore the matter. And I did not want to offend an important man like yourself. So I came in person. Mrs. Morgan has already assured me it must be a malicious practical joke. Good-day, Mrs. Morgan. Good-day, sir."

And we left the apartment, without another word being spoken. It was not until we were again in the Commissioner's car, on our way back to Headquarters, that Thatcher Colt spoke:

"How did a fine woman like that ever marry such a creature?"

And then, after a moment's pause, he added:

"Why should Humphrey Maskell want to kill Geraldine Foster? If he wanted to kill anybody, there was a ready-made victim for him right at hand in the person of his beloved's husband."

17

THE BOY WITH THE BUCK TEETH

I think the Geraldine Foster case really began to be solved that night. More, I think the first glimmer of the final solution came to Thatcher Colt as, an hour after dinner, we left Police Headquarters, and walked down the vaulted passage-way, the echo of our footsteps resounding down the range of pillared arches. I knew that Thatcher Colt's mind was still busy arranging a conspectus of the various puzzling features in the case, as we entered the department car and Neil McMahon received a brief instruction where to take us.

"So far as the public is concerned," said Colt, suddenly breaking silence, "Dougherty has a more convincing case than ever. He can smell Doctor Maskell burning in the electric chair. The victim—a girl, the standard bearer of American womanhood, fighting to save her honor. The accused—the pampered son of a very wealthy man, the heir to millions of dollars. This is Dougherty's opportunity to be Governor of New York. He will pawn his soul to prove Maskell guilty. What a *bonne bouche* it would be for the reporters, if they knew what we were up to—they would scream in headlines that Dougherty and I were in a death struggle for political honors. Not one reporter would be willing to believe that the only motive in the mind of the Police Commissioner was to see justice done."

And, after a moment, he added, with a chuckle:

"Yet I took the trouble to ask Doctor Maskell for the name of his barber! And he did not even thank me!"

By this time we had reached the outlying frontiers of Greenwich Village. At the place where Fourth Street crosses Seventh Avenue in the drunken crisscross of the Village highways, we left the car and proceeded on foot. The Commissioner led half-way down the block to a thick round pole, painted with red and white stripes, and surmounted by the blue globe of an electric light—the signpost of a basement barber shop. We descended and found the shop deserted of customers. The barber, a diminutive Italian with black curls, volcanic eyes and an impertinent black mustache, was reading an account of Doctor Maskell's arrest in the New York *Evening Graphic*.

Calmly, Thatcher Colt sat down in the chair and asked for a hair trim and shave while I slouched in a chair and fingered a copy of *Liberty* magazine.

"Good evening!" said the barber, adjusting a cloth around the neck of the Police Commissioner. "It is a very nice night."

This point Thatcher Colt conceded with affable good nature. Encouraged by his friendly customer, Marinelli, the barber, like so many of his tribe, became talkative, and launched into a bitter denunciation of the new traffic system, never dreaming that its author lay just beneath his razor. The Police Commissioner, by grunts and other sounds, continued to agree with him through the lather. But at the first opportunity, Colt managed to defend his office by pointing to the efficiency of the Department in clearing up the Foster murder.

"Ah," said the barber, "but that is too very sad."

"Sad? How so?"

"That Doctor Maskell. He is one of my best customers. He come here often. He is one fine man. But he is cursed by charm. He is too damn attractive to the girls."

Thatcher Colt nodded under the lifted blade.

"It's a great way to be cursed sometimes," he jested.

"No. It was the doctor's ruin. Poor doctor. The women followed him."

"Followed him?"

"Yes, yes. Even into my shop they followed him."

I bent low over the magazine I pretended to read.

"So the women followed the doctor into this very place!" exclaimed the Police Commissioner.

"One did. She just wanted to be near him—she admitted it."

Who could this woman have been? The same mysterious creature the doctor had found at his office door? The one who had telephoned him through Mrs. Westock and summoned him to the house on Peddler's Road?

"What excuse did she have for coming in to your shop—was she here for a manicure?" asked Colt.

"Yes, but that was a bluff—she liked the doctor."

"Pretty girl?" asked the Commissioner carelessly.

"Not so young—very pretty—not so bad," chortled the voluble barber. "Blonde hair, nice shape, sweet voice. Just a married woman—I saw the ring—just a married woman with a yearning, devouring, searing—ah! ah! terrific passion for a strong, good-looking man. She said she did not even know his name. But she confessed her feeling to me.

"And you took pity on her?"

"Yes—I gave her a lock of his hair, after he went out."

The Commissioner laughed. No one could have guessed from his easy attitude, that now the hunter had sniffed a scent—I lit a cigarette to hide my own deep excitement.

"Does she come here often?"

The barber shook his head.

"No, she never came back. Why? You are not that silly lady's husband?"

He drew back. With the natural dramatic instinct of his race, he was ready to make a tragedy out of any conversation he got into.

"No," said Thatcher Colt. "But I am a friend of Doctor Maskell. I am one of the few men in the city today who believes him innocent."

"Si, signor."

"The lady wore a wedding ring. What did it look like?"

The barber's liquid eyes turned upward in turmoil.

"The ring," he said at last, "was of platinum—set with diamonds—and two big pearls."

"Thanks."

The barber shrugged his shoulders.

"Shampoo? Massage?"

Thatcher Colt, who remained silent while the final touches were given his face and hair, had one question held in reserve. He put it casually, as he rose from the chair.

"Would you know that woman if you saw her again?" he asked.

The barber looked at the Commissioner's face and for the first time really recognized him.

"Mother of God!" he whispered. "The Commissioner!"

"Could you identify that woman, Marinelli?"

"Yes—yes."

"And you can keep your mouth shut?"

"Ah—I am a man of few words, Mr. Commissioner!"

We emerged into the darkness of the street.

"Now," said Thatcher Colt, a few minutes later, when we were again in the car and driving uptown, "it is becoming more and more apparent that the killer had no real grudge against Geraldine Foster. That poor girl was merely a pawn to be sacrificed in a larger game, in which millions were involved. All the evidence planted against the doctor is leading to that conclusion. Imagine collecting the doctor's hair cuttings, just to fake the refuse under the dead girl's finger nails."

We came to a halt in front of a walk-up apartment on upper Broadway, not far from the scene of the crime. Thatcher Colt calmly mounted four flights of steps and rapped on the door. A woman, in her nightgown, just about to go to bed, and with a baby feeding at her left breast, opened the door and stared at us with dull resentment.

"Mrs. Planzen?"

"Yeh."

"Has your little boy gone to bed?"

"What's he been doin'?"

"Nothing. I want to talk with him. I want to reward him, in fact."

"Oh, yeh? And who are you?"

"I'm from the Police," said Thatcher Colt, in his friendliest voice. "I talked with your young man for a few minutes the other day, and I took his name and address, and now I want to talk with him again."

The woman kicked the door with her foot, but Colt was too quick for her and his foot was thrust out in time to stop it from closing.

"Now, Mrs. Planzen, you are not in any trouble. It happens that your little boy plays near Peddler's Road and I am hoping he can help me in a very important case."

"Oh, gee, mom, lemme talk to him!" and there came under the mother's elbow, the same sallow-faced, buck-toothed urchin who ran from me that cold day when Betty Canfield and I first came upon the house on Peddler's Road.

"Helloa, Warren," said the Commissioner, who never forgets a name once he has heard it. 'You remember me?"

"Sure."

Turning to his mother, he pleaded:

"Aw, let him come in, mom. They're cops, but they don't care nothing about the apple jack in our kitchen. They're just Tammany Hall guys."

We did our best to keep a straight face, as Mrs. Planzen said:

"Any reward that would go to my child comes to his mother what needs it to keep soul and body together—and not to his father who drinks up every cent that he lays his hands on."

"Exactly," agreed Thatcher Colt, and presently we were admitted into the shabby little living room.

"Now, Warren," he said, "before I went inside the house that other day, you told me a wild story about a ghost without any clothes in the murder house?"

"Yes, sir."

"What made you say that?"

"I saw it."

"You saw the naked ghost?"

"Yes, sir."

"Where?"

"Inside the house."

"Where were you?"

"I was inside the house, too."

"When was that?"

"Christmas Eve."

"What were you doing up there?"

The boy turned first red and then white and hung his head.

"You don't remember," said Mrs. Planzen, who was distrustful of police honor.

"It's all right," the Commissioner told him. "I am not going to harm you."

"I broke in the house," confessed the boy. "But I didn't mean to steal anything. I was just playing robber's cave."

"Anybody with you?"

"No, sir."

"Did you break the window?"

"No, sir. That was broke a long time ago."

"Did you find anybody in there?"

"No, sir—not right off. It was all awful quiet. I was pretty cold. I stayed in the kitchen for a while, trying to get up the nerve to light the gas stove. Then I heard a noise and I got awful scared, and I was ashamed of that and finally, just to prove to myself that I wasn't scared at all, I sneaked up the back stairs. It was getting dark and I could hardly see my way and I walked on my toes. When I got upstairs, I was still more scared,—I don't know why, but I was sure there was somebody up there—I was afraid to go upstairs or down, either—so I jumped to the window in the hall and climbed out on the window sill. I let myself down by my hands when I saw it coming down the hall."

"Saw what?"

"The ghost."

"What was it like?"

"It didn't have any clothes on and it was all covered with blood.

"Warren, was it a man or a woman?"

"It was a lady," answered the boy, beginning to whimper.

"A hell of a lady," said his mother, "even if she was murdered."

"What did you do then?"

"I ran home."

"Did you tell your mother?"

"Not a word," said Mrs. Planzen bitterly. And the ill-favored look she gave Warren boded ill for the presidential namesake's peace after our departure.

"Is that all you know about the case?" persisted Thatcher Colt. "Did you see anything else up there?"

"No, sir. I went back the next day, but I didn't see anything. I was afraid to go in any more. But I liked to hang around—that is why you found me the day you came up there."

When we emerged from the house, Thatcher Colt was very thoughtful. At the corner, he stopped and chatted with the patrolman stationed there—a youthful police-man, almost inarticulate on finding himself face to face with the Commissioner.

"Is there a locksmith near here?" Thatcher Colt asked him.

"Yes—right there," the patrolman replied, pointing to a basement shop across the street. A light was still burning in its tiny window.

The locksmith was a thin, weazened old man with dark glasses.

"Ever see that before?" asked Thatcher Colt, throwing down the old-fashioned key with the blue ribbon.

"I made it."

"For whom?"

"A lady. I don't know her name."

"Describe her."

The description given by the locksmith differed slight-ly from the one furnished by the barber, in coloring, size, and general impression. But the method of obtaining the key, as the man narrated it, seemed greatly to interest the Commissioner. The woman had come to his shop and tak-en the locksmith up the hill and to the house on Peddler's Road. The door was standing open. It was fitted with an old-fashioned lock and the woman said the key was lost. Could he make her another? As Colt pointed out, she must have first burglarized the house through the broken kitch-en window. The mechanic removed the lock, took it back to the shop, found an old key which he fitted, came back and refitted the lock into the front door, all in the space of a few hours.

"Thanks," said Thatcher Colt, making a memorandum of the name and address. "You will hear from me later."

Again we drove downtown and this time we stopped in front of the Esplanade Apartments on Morningside Heights. A strange thrill stirred in my veins as I mounted the stone steps. This was once the dwelling place of a girl whose death we still sought to solve, but also it was, until recently, the home of another girl who had come to dominate my thoughts. But Betty had moved from here now and was living on Tenth Street.

Promptly Thatcher Colt sought out our old acquaintance, the janitor. Still sagging, as if he were sitting on an invisible stool, and still in his ragged clothing, the janitor received us sullenly.

"Who showed Apartment 4-D to prospective tenants?" was the Commissioner's question.

We were referred to the elevator operator. He explained that a sign had been hung out stating that an apartment was for sub-let. But the Christmas season was bad for new rentals and there had been only one person interested.

"Do you remember who it was?" asked Thatcher Colt.

The elevator operator remembered perfectly.

"It was a lady," he said, "with blue eyes and blonde hair."

Blue eyes and blonde hair! To whom was this leading us?

"Can you remember the woman more accurately?"

"Well, she was about as tall as your friend there."

I am about five feet nine inches tall.

"Was she pretty?"

"I didn't get a good look at her face," said the operator. "She kept her coat muffled up about her face both times she was here."

"Oh, she was here twice?"

"Yes. The first time she came about two or three weeks before Christmas. The girls were not at home, but I showed her around."

"Did you leave her alone in the apartment?"

"Well—"

"You are not supposed to, but you did. Is that right?"

"Yes."

Thatcher Colt turned to me with an amused smile.

"You see," he said, "that was the time the lady had the opportunity to steal the pen and some of the paper."

"Nothing was ever reported missing," protested the boy, but Thatcher Colt waved that aside.

"When did she come again?"

"About two o'clock in the afternoon of Christmas Eve. She said she thought she would take the apartment, but she wanted another chance to look at it."

"The apartment being vacant was a stroke of luck for the lady we are after," muttered the Commissioner. "This time she brought back the torn piece of the note she had forged. You see, Tony, we have to reckon with the fact that this woman was clever enough to be a forger. Probably she obtained a sample of Geraldine's writing as Geraldine's mysterious correspondent, wanting genealogical informa-tion. And she planted those torn papers on the second visit. Then she went down to Doctor Maskell's suite—and I wonder what happened there?"

I left Thatcher Colt at his home and went to my own bachelor quarters for some needed sleep. The next day Thatcher Colt occupied himself with affairs that were an enigma to me.

Early in the morning, he sent for Clesleek, his favor-ite among the chemists attached to the department, and had a long consultation with him. But I knew nothing of the business of that interview until midnight. I did no-tice, however, that when Clesleek left the Commissioner's office, he carried with him a sealed envelope, that in his hand was a small red object, trimmed with gold, and that he promised to see the perfumers.

But I had no time to speculate. There were stacks of neglected department work on my desk; the Foster case had taken much of my time, while I served as aide-de-camp to the Commissioner. Yet now it was hard for me to concentrate. All my interest lay in the new developments in the murder mystery. Nor did it lessen my curiosity when Thatcher Colt paused by my desk later in the afternoon, and rested a hand confidentially on my shoulder.

"I am beginning to see daylight at last, Tony," he divulged. "There is only one thing left to bother me."

He patted his hands together and walked out of the room, his somber brown eyes fixed in a stare like that of a medium in a trance. Sometimes, when Thatcher Colt was thus moody and silent, it seemed to me that he drew upon some intangible power of inspiration, or illumination, to light up the dark corners of vexing crimes. But he stoutly scouts the possibility of such phenomena. Logic and observation explain it all, he declares.

Nevertheless, I do not believe that logic explains all that Thatcher Colt discovered as he grappled with that invisible antagonist who had, apparently, sought in the murder of Geraldine Foster, to perpetrate the perfect crime—and had very nearly succeeded.

I was deep in my work, when suddenly Thatcher Colt returned and again touched me on the shoulder.

"Tony," he said, "stop your work."

I looked up and he smiled whimsically.

"I have the honor to report," he said, "that I have finally solved the Geraldine Foster murder case."

18

I KNOW WHO KILLED GERALDINE FOSTER

A strange meeting was held that night at the house on West Seventieth Street.

So extraordinary was the gathering that, had they known, the reporters would have descended *en masse* on the house of the Commissioner, frantic at the whispered reports of new developments in the Foster case. No one would tell what was afoot, nor did they learn that all the witnesses had been hurriedly summoned and were now corralled in one of the chambers on the second floor of the Commissioner's house. Among them were Mr. and Mrs. Foster and their adopted son, Bruce, together with Betty Canfield, Harry Armstrong, Mrs. Haberhorn and several others who would not have been recognized by the reporters at all—especially a boy with buck teeth,—a voluble and protesting Italian barber, and a locksmith. The doors of the house were guarded by patrolmen.

But an infinitely stranger gathering was held in the library of the Police Commissioner.

In front of the desk sat George Maskell, prim and precise, his finger tips together, his chin lost in his huge, upstanding collar. Across from him sat his wife, Natalie, looking pale and august and beautiful. Between them, grim and thoughtful, slouched the prisoner, Doctor Humphrey Maskell.

Facing this embattled trio stood District Attorney Merle Dougherty, his pudgy hands clasped behind his back, his red curls rumpled, his blue eyes glittering. Dougherty refused to sit down but stalked angrily back and forth as if he found it difficult to contain his indignation at these bizarre and unnecessary proceedings. His marching raised a wind that fluttered the leaves of my note-book, as I sat waiting to make a record of all that was said and done.

Tranquil and mysterious, looking somberly upon them all, Thatcher Colt suddenly appeared at the little private door.

"Good evening," said the Commissioner, standing by his desk. Before any one could reply, Dougherty declared himself.

"I want to say," he blurted, "that I regard this entire proceeding as entirely irregular. Why are we here?"

As Thatcher Colt busied himself with his pipe, be replied, "To rehearse, step by step, the murder of Geraldine Foster—and to accuse the actual criminal—whom I now have safely under lock and key."

Dougherty's face flushed an even deeper red.

"Then we are wasting time. The actual criminal is under arrest," he snarled. "If Doctor Maskell is not, as I understand it, prepared to make a confession—"

"Confess to what?" interrupted Natalie Maskell, with spirit. "We have made it very plain that our client confesses to nothing."

Dougherty glared at the "she-lawyer," as he once called her, with a belligerent air.

"Sit down, Dougherty," counselled Thatcher Colt, in a placating tone, "and let me explain."

With his left arm slung up over the back of the chair, and his blue eyes fixed like a sentinel's on the pale and impassive face of the prisoner, Dougherty blinked and sat down.

"Shoot!" he exploded, inelegantly.

"I know who killed Geraldine Foster," began Thatcher Colt promptly. His quiet voice was free from all excitement. "I know how Geraldine was killed, and why. I am prepared to prove every statement I make, as I lead you after the killer from the start to the finish of this bloody business."

He now turned his attention directly to Dougherty.

"I will first tell you about Doctor Maskell," he said. "The doctor is the victim of an unfortunate marriage. He has never tried to free himself from this vixenish and parasitic woman—until he fell in love with Felise Morgan. Her marriage, too, was unfortunate—but she stayed on, out of pity and loyalty to her mother-in-law. It is true that this man and this woman sinned in the eyes of a conventional world. But that was the only offense Doctor Maskell committed—except that he left for Reno, meaning to make preliminary arrangements and return for Felise, her little girl and her mother-in-law. He intended defraying all expenses, procuring a double divorce, to be followed by a marriage. That was the reason this crime was committed."

All of us drew our chairs a little closer then. The three Maskells looked at Thatcher Colt with expressions of puzzled and eager interest, and anxious unanimity of emotion. Only Dougherty sulked.

"The killer of Geraldine Foster," resumed Colt, "did not know her. Slayer and victim were unacquainted. They were total strangers. They had no reason to love or hate each other."

The rim of four faces, turned toward Thatcher Colt, became as images of puzzled wonder. What kind of mad theory was the Police Commissioner about to suggest?

"The motive was one free of all animosity. Hate did not enter into the crime. Neither did love, jealousy, or fear. None of the grand emotions played a part. There was never a case that was less of a crime of passion than this. The murder of Geraldine Foster was a cold-blooded, mathematical proposition."

"A cold-blooded axe-murder," fleered Dougherty. "That's a good one."

But Thatcher Colt went calmly on: "From the outset, there were three major questions in this murder. They were, as I stated, in the beginning:

"Why did the murderer use an axe?

"Why was the corpse denuded of all its clothing, except for a pillow case over the head?

"Who was the mysterious woman who met Doctor Maskell at his office door, within an hour after the murder was done?"

Having recited these three riddles, Thatcher Colt threw back his head and permitted a plume of lavender tobacco smoke to spiral upward from his lips, like the nebula of a new world in the process of being born.

"Those questions I had set myself to answer," he continued. "They were vital because they were so utterly idiocratic. They stamped the crime at once as peculiar and unique,—making this deed different from all other dark deeds with which I am familiar. Through them I felt certain I could grope my way to all the other necessary facts."

"And did you?" asked George Maskell keenly.

"I did. I will begin with the earliest planning of the crime and see to what it leads us. We will call our criminal simply 'X'. We must be prepared to assume that 'X' is a person with a lust for money, a mania quite as common as any other mental disorder, but not as well recognized as in the past, when we had honest misers, and portrayed them in melodrama. Remember that 'X' is money crazy, for, gentlemen, the murder of Geraldine Foster was done for money and nothing else."

I could feel a cold chill crawling like a living creature through my veins. The single statement of Thatcher Colt was horrible beyond credence.

"How do you know that?" asked Natalie Maskell. "It is an interesting, but hardly plausible, theory."

"It is the logic of the whole evidence. I put it first, but I found it last."

"I would like to hear the facts first," purred Dougherty, with covert sarcasm.

"Nevertheless, you will assume with me that our unknown character, 'X', was money crazy. Some time within the last two years, 'X' suddenly conceived a brilliant scheme. It had a touch of genius, which is to say, of madness. By the death of Geraldine Foster, 'X' foresaw gain. The temptation must have been—no, plainly it was—irresistible.

"I do not know how long it took to hatch this cunning and blood-thirsty notion. But I am sure that even the most consummate schemer would be unable to lay it out in all its perfect detail without months, perhaps years of thought. For it was put together with the patient perfection of Chinese puzzle boxes. Finally, it all fitted. The scheme was complete. It was ready for execution."

"So far, all sheer assumption!" remarked Dougherty.

"For the accomplishment of this crime, it became necessary for 'X' to obtain a sample of the handwriting of Geraldine Foster. This was elaborately managed. Out of the West came a letter for Geraldine Foster,—a single genealogical inquiry from one Mr. Ephraim Foster. Apparently some old fanatic on the subject of the Foster family tree was trying to trace its branches and to him Geraldine was a new twig. In his very first letter he assured her that she was descended from a line of kings. Fascinated by the thought that she had royal blood in her veins, Geraldine replied to the letter. Several exchanges followed—and then Geraldine heard from the genealogist no more. All her letters were returned.

"Now it happens that I was able to find the original letter to Geraldine Foster from Ephraim Foster. Geraldine had turned it over to her parents, as they were curious about it, too. With this clue in my hand, I sent a wire to the chief of police in the little town of Willoughby, Kansas, from which the letter came. Through the local police, I had the post-office box traced. Thus I learned, with considerable amazement, that the box was rented in the Willoughby post office by a transient visitor to a nearby town—one who came there about five months ago, stayed a few weeks, and then departed, suddenly and mysteriously, never to be heard from again, and leaving no forwarding address. That was in August of last year.

"But from the post-master I was at least able to obtain a description of the character whom we now know as 'X' and also as Ephraim Foster,—a description which may have been vague but which was nevertheless astounding.

"For the post-master at Willoughby, Kansas, declared that the so-called Ephraim Foster was a woman!

"You look surprised. Will you feel more astonished if I tell you I was not surprised. That I had expected to find that the genealogist who wrote Geraldine wore skirts.

"When you know all the story, you will know that from my first examination of the house on Peddler's Road, I suspected that the murderer did not dress as a man. And already a suspicion of who this clever 'X' might be leaped into my mind—for I was told that the one person to whom I might ascribe a motive—a woman—was out of New York during all August.

"My suspicions were not deeply founded at this early stage of the game. Now I can tell you with definite assurance that by this elaborate and fantastic genealogical device, 'X' had obtained copious samples of the writing of Geraldine Foster. For what purpose? Obviously in preparation for a forgery. I do not have to tell any of you here—with the possible exception of Doctor Maskell—that forgery is by no means the rare and delicate accomplishment generally supposed. Expert forgery need mean no more than the power to draw accurately. I know many artists who can imitate perfectly any signature at the first trial. I have since proved that the person whom I had begun to suspect was 'X' studied drawing, many years ago. I have been shown samples of 'X's work.

"Between August and December 24, 'X' had ample time to copy the handwriting of Geraldine Foster.

"Meanwhile, luck favored the plotter. I do not know to what sly resources 'X' would have fallen if chance had not smiled upon those dark plans. Geraldine Foster was about to be married. Therefore she was leaving the apartment on Morningside Heights, and Betty Canfield was seeking smaller quarters for herself. The apartment was for sublet. The girls worked during the day and 'X' called to look at the apartment during the day.

"For what purpose? On the first occasion, 'X' stole stationery and a pen—but overlooked one important detail. All purple inks are not the same. That aroused my first suspicion in the case. The note which demanded blackmail money from Doctor Maskell was a forged note. It was brought back to the apartment on Morningside Heights by 'X' who, left alone in the living room, tore it across and thrust the pieces into the desk drawer, certain that later on they would be found. If they had not been found, 'X' would have planted the fragments of a second note. Nothing was to be left to chance. But it happened that the scheme worked perfectly the first time. Again it was lucky that Betty Canfield saw Geraldine half-finish a note and then destroy it—which threw us all off the track, until our detectives found the fragments of both notes. It was also on the second visit that the key to the house on Peddler's Road was left in Geraldine's coat.

"We know that this was not the only note written by 'X'. Another was completed and instead of being torn up was sent directly to Felise Morgan, the mother of Doris. The purpose of this was manifest. It was to create even in the mind of Doctor Maskell's nearest and dearest a doubt of his innocence, and to show to the police the ostensible motive for the deed. Further, the note also showed us where to look for the body,—it gave us our first intimation of the house on Peddler's Road—serving two deadly purposes."

Natalie Maskell smiled in admiration.

"It is marvelous how you have worked this out, Mr. Colt," she said. "I am beginning to be afraid that you have anticipated the very defense we have been preparing, and which absolutely clears my brother-in-law."

"But your husband does not seem so confident," sneered Dougherty. The District Attorney was still entirely unimpressed by Thatcher Colt's reconstruction of the case. And in this instance Dougherty had spoken shrewdly. Old George Maskell, the lion of the court rooms of New York, looked depressed. His eyes were like the windows of an empty house. Yet he answered the remark of Dougherty directly and forcefully.

"I'm listening to all that is said," he replied. "I will reply at the proper time."

"Also," interrupted Natalie, "you have not explained why Humphrey was selected as the victim of this mysterious 'X'. Why all these devilish preparations?"

Thatcher Colt smiled mysteriously.

"That will presently appear," he said. "Doctor Maskell was the only possible victim in this case. 'X' had also been busy finding out about the private affairs of the doctor during the autumn. Everything that he would wish to keep hidden had been found out by this prying 'X'. He had been followed to the house on Peddler's Road, and his secret love affair was known.

"I learned that 'X' had burglarized the house on Peddler's Road, got inside and studied the layout of the little house. More than that, 'X' had sent for a locksmith and had a private key made for the front door. The locksmith, by the way, is now under this same roof with us. 'X' could come and go in the house at whim, so long as the doctor and his friend were not there.

"Therefore, 'X' had contrived free access to the stage on which the coming drama of blood was to be played. And, while lurking in that house, 'X's' all-seeing eyes had fallen upon Doctor Maskell's axe.

"Even then, the preparations for this astounding crime were not complete. 'X' must add a final touch of horror, to seal the doctor's doom. By now, you must begin to see that Geraldine Foster was only an incident in the scheme. The doctor was to be the real victim. His was the death that was to be encompassed, and the State would do the killing. 'X' would commit the murder of the girl. No one would see. Then 'X' must preserve the dead body against decay until it would be possible further to entangle Doctor Maskell. That might be days—even a week—yet when the body was found, it must have the appearance of being freshly killed. Tannic acid would do that. The idea was filched from an old murder in New Jersey with which I am, as well as 'X' was, familiar. The plan was clearly defined—kill, put the body in the tub, soak it in the preservative, and leave it there. Later, one could go back, bury the body, and then contrive by some device to involve the doctor with a difficulty in proving his movements. But he must not get into the house, otherwise he would discover what had happened, perhaps notify the police himself, and thus rub off some of the sheen of suspicion which 'X' was so carefully polishing in all the contrived circumstances. Here was a real problem, unique in crime, I believe, yet 'X' met it with consummate skill.

"Accordingly, the murder was committed on Christmas Eve in the afternoon exactly as scheduled. I will give you the details of this in just a minute. But let me leap ahead for a moment. A few days after Christmas, Doctor Maskell leaves town suddenly, mysteriously, without an explanation. Why? 'X' knew perfectly well—the secret trip to Reno preparatory to getting a divorce. It was this romance which hastened the crime. All of these plans, coincidental as they may seem at first glance really show why the crime was committed at just this time. 'X' seized the opportunity because it was necessary. If Felise and the doctor were married, the reason for the crime itself would cease to be.

"'X' knew that the doctor would return on January 4. In the meantime, no one would be visiting the house on Peddler's Road. Therefore, all that time the body of Geraldine Foster lay washing in the tub of tannic acid. But on the night of January 3, some one in the neighborhood is willing to testify they saw a light in the house. That was the night 'X' returned there and buried the body, single-handed.

"Therefore the Medical Examiner was right when he said the body had been in the grave for thirty-six hours. But the pigeons had given me a clue, which the autopsy substantiated. The girl had been in the grave thirty-six hours but she was killed on December 24. It had been the design of 'X' to make it seem that Geraldine had been killed on January 3, when Doctor Maskell could not account for his movements. Here great cleverness came into play.

"'X' figured that the doctor could be lured to some place where he had no means of proving that he was, then the police would believe that he was lying, and the full result would be accomplished. Accordingly, on January 4, he received a telephone call. He was told that it was Geraldine Foster talking—he believed it—and he was further told that if he would come to her at once he could save her from great trouble. She seemed ready to commit suicide. The doctor was an impulsive man and went to keep the assignation. He said that he was to meet her at the Pelham entrance to Bronx Park. He went there and waited two hours and saw no one. But such was his isolated position that no one who knew him saw him there.

"That made the doctor's story look fishy to us, and the District Attorney wisely laid stress on it, just as 'X' intended he should.

"But the tannic acid ruse had not worked. It never does. The Medical Examiners, when they make the autopsy, are certain sooner or later to discover the fraud. And then, the snails in the stomach of Geraldine Foster were conclusive. It might have looked as if all this magnificent plot of 'X' had failed, or at least the prepared case against the doctor greatly weakened, simply because the police almost instantly found out the exact time of the murder.

"But here that strange element of chance which had played against the real killer now changed sides and helped in the plot. We knew that Geraldine Foster had been killed on Christmas Eve. But that did not help the doctor, for his Christmas Eve alibi was just as defective as the one of January 4. The killer had first meant to lure him there directly, in which case no tannic acid would have been necessary. After Mrs. Westock delivered the message, the doctor called Mrs. Morgan—because he was suspicious. They arranged to meet, but the husband returned unexpectedly and Mrs. Morgan could not leave her apartment. Doctor Maskell, in an auction room, had no alibi, and he would not betray the lady when we questioned him about

it. We had to find her through the pillow case which had
been deliberately put over the head of the victim, because
the killer remembered the Anna Aumüller case and knew
exactly what the police would do with that."

"A gruesome enough scheme," remarked George Maskell, with a glance at the Police Commissioner.

"'X' decided to leave nothing to chance. If anything
went wrong with the tannic acid, it must be shown that
Doctor Maskell had tried to fix an alibi for himself, and
that he bought the chemical. Accordingly, at the proper
time, a telephone call was made to the Wisner pharmacy.
The druggist was told that Doctor Maskell wished three
large bottles of tannic acid, and they must be delivered
before two o'clock in the afternoon. This was done, and
two of those bottles, missing from the doctor's office,
were found in the brush near the house on Peddler's Road.
Moreover, a witness was found who saw Geraldine Foster
leaving the office carrying these two bottles—her own em-
balming fluid."

"How horrible and fantastic—almost unbelievable, Mr.
Commissioner," said Natalie Maskell.

"At a little after three o'clock that, afternoon, 'X'
arrived at the office of Doctor Maskell. I do not know
what passed between those two, but it is not hard to guess.
A woman came to Geraldine Foster with a pretended message, a summons from Doctor Maskell. She accompanied
that woman, bringing the bottles which the doctor had
requested—and thus was led to her place of execution. It
must have been something urgent to impress the mind of
Geraldine Foster—so much so that she agreed to go with
this stranger, carrying those bottles with her. In a private
car they drove uptown. So much we know. Now we have
to draw again upon our telepathic or deductive powers.
'X' and Geraldine entered the house. No sooner was the
door closed than the woman bade Geraldine sit down and

wait. The woman went upstairs, taking the bottles. There she emptied them into the tub and turned the spigot on. But no identifiable thumb prints or finger prints show on the highly polished spigot. The woman had clearly put on gloves.

"Now, this mysterious woman did an appalling thing—and for a highly practical reason. She took off every stitch of clothing and came down stairs naked, axe in hand.

"Perhaps you have guessed why the murderess elected to do her awful deed while she herself was naked. There was a lot of blood flying through the dark air of that little house. Her clothes must not be spattered. So she was nude, and afterward she stood in the shower and washed herself."

"Good God!" breathed Dougherty, crossing himself.

"At the time exactly fixed by the battered wristwatch, 'X', the blood-thirsty woman, without warning fell upon poor Geraldine Foster with the axe. The girl was literally hacked to death—probably not until after many blows was her skull crushed. Her screams were unheard. There was a furious struggle. The room showed that plainly enough when at last we got there. But the deed was done. Geraldine Foster was killed.

"Lifting the still warm and bloody body, the naked murderess carried it upstairs and laid it on the bathroom floor. Crossing then to the upstairs bedroom because she heard a noise, 'X' encountered an apparition. A boy was looking in at her from the hall window. The room was dark. Identification was hardly possible. Nevertheless, someone had seen. Instantly the clever mind of this mad creature worked out the solution. The boy turned and fled, but the woman fell to work. The body would be stripped anyhow, for the soaking in the tub. But before burial 'X' would have dressed it again, had it not been for this accident. Instead, the body was buried nude, and if that boy ever testified, he would believe that it was Geraldine he saw, and not the murderess.

"That was the reason Geraldine Foster was found nude, and her blood-soaked clothes found in the dark corner of the closet in Doctor Maskell's suite. The murderess put them there. She drove back to Washington Square and opened that office with Geraldine's key. She carried the clothes inside and planted them where they would eventually be found, and hung the coat and purse conspicuously on a hook. Then she came out of the office, locked the door and was about to leave when suddenly—and here I guess—she remembered having left something inside. She had to wait until the doctor came before she came in—and she ran a fearful risk of recognition. The doctor, however, did not recognize her—it was dark and there was another reason, too.

"But my friends, the woman will be recognized. I found traces which led me to her by devious but certain steps. The first clue was a hair from a woman's head. I have it here."

From his desk drawer, Thatcher Colt drew out two envelopes, both marked with the word "Hair". We watched with fascinated interest. The tale he had told us had stirred us all deeply. Dougherty was the first to bend over the desk, his face washed free of all cheapness of jealousy, almost of all doubt, indeed, as he leaned on his elbows to see what Thatcher Colt had now to show. Natalie Maskell and her husband were keen and alert. Even Doctor Maskell stirred from his deep lethargy, leaned forward, and watched.

"This first envelope," said Colt, holding it up, "contains a hair I took from the hair-net of Geraldine Foster the night I first visited her apartment. I kept it because I thought I might need it if her body were found and identification proved difficult. This other hair I found on the floor, where it had fallen from the head of the murderess, probably during the struggle."

Opening the second envelope, Colt drew out a long almost invisible strand of hair. It was of a medium blonde.

"I may tell you," added the Commissioner, "that the murderess has since had her hair dyed. If you look among all the possible suspects, you will not find the counterpart of this hair. But now I will show you a third exhibit."

The silence was almost deafening in its effect as Thatcher Colt drew out a third envelope. Then from a lower, deeper drawer, he took out a long, thin glass tube on a low pedestal, a hydrostatic tube such as is used by chemists. It was filled with a colorless liquid.

"Recently," explained Colt, "I managed by stealth to obtain several hairs from the head of the woman I suspect of killing Geraldine Foster. I took a leaf from her own book—I went to her own beauty parlor and bribed a girl there—just as she had gone to Doctor Maskell's barber, and obtained a cutting for an equally deadly purpose. Here is one of her hairs—a dark and lovely auburn. But observe when I drop it into this chemical that the dye falls away." We watched that demonstration in utter silence. The tiny strand of hair fell almost unseen into the chemical, and then the water became discolored. After a moment Thatcher Colt drew out the hair and dropped it across his sleeve and beside it he laid the one found on the scene of the crime.

They were a perfect match.

"Good God!" cried Dougherty again. "Who is this woman, Colt?"

The Police Commissioner shrugged his shoulders.

"Even such an identification as this might not convince a jury," he temporized, "but fortunately I found another. In the bathroom of the murder-house was a face cloth. It had scarlet stains on it. They might have been taken for blood stains, but they were not. They were the stains of a lipstick. At some cost to the department, I had those stains analyzed—a delicate and lengthy task—and I compared them with the dried pieces of lipstick taken from the lips of Geraldine Foster—they had been fixed there in a crust by the tannic acid. I found that the lipstick used by Geraldine Foster was a Corday product, but the one used by the murderess was from Coty.

George Maskell nodded his head tragically.

"And you have found the Coty lipstick on the woman you suspect?" he asked in a strange voice.

"I have," said Thatcher Colt. "I observed her stick one day when she dropped it in this very room."

Natalie Maskell, rising, was pale as snow and smiling strangely.

"Do you accuse me of murdering Geraldine Foster?" she cried.

"I do," said Thatcher Colt. "And you did it with an axe because no one would connect a woman with such a weapon!"

George Maskell struggled pathetically to his feet, an old and beaten man, and tried to take his stand beside his wife. Dougherty, too, stood up, staring unbelievingly into the face of this calm woman, this banshee, scorning the rest of us, even in this hour of terrible disclosure. Doctor Maskell stared up at her in horror, but she had eyes only for Thatcher Colt.

"I have sat here and listened, divining to what you were leading," she mocked. "But I have yet to hear the motive."

"Your father-in-law has not long to live. He will bequeath millions of dollars to each of his two sons. But if one son dies, the other gets all. You wanted all. You are mad—money-mad," said Thatcher Colt, in solemn and accusing tones.

She laughed balefully.

"You are very clever, Mr. Colt," she cried, "but you must admit it was a pretty plan."

"To have the State kill the man you wanted to get rid of? It is a clever, but not a new device."

"Indeed? But you have not won yet, Mr. Colt." And Natalie Maskell sat down and began to laugh, most horribly, shaking her shoulders and quivering. Divining her terrible meaning, Thatcher Colt rushed to the medicine cabinet in his dressing room, while Humphrey Maskell sprang to the side of the woman who would have destroyed him. But she was already beyond the need of a doctor—and not one of us had noticed when she swallowed the poison tablet, half-way through Colt's explanation.

By the time Thatcher Colt had returned, the murderess of Geraldine Foster lay, beautiful and unconscious, on the floor. An hour later she was dead.

19

THE FINISH

To the astonishment of all New York, on the following day Doctor Humphrey Maskell was suddenly released from the Tombs. The indictment against him was quashed, the case stetted, and Dougherty made a handsome statement in which he completely exonerated the laughing physician of Washington Square.

"Then, who did kill Geraldine Foster?" howled the newspapers. "What is going on behind the scenes of the District Attorney's and the Police Commissioner's offices?"

They never knew. The facts were rigidly withheld. They are given here now because the principals who would have suffered needlessly from the publication of the facts are beyond all harm. George Maskell, a broken man, has at last been laid in his grave, solaced until the last by the knowledge that the terrible crime of the woman he had trusted was never revealed.

As he went to her funeral, I could see by the look he fixed on the coffin that he realized the truth. If Natalie Maskell had succeeded in her terrible design, it would have been only a little while before her own husband would have been the next victim. Then all the money would have been hers. As it was, she was the first to be buried.

Doctor Humphrey Maskell and the beautiful woman he loved are thousands of leagues from Washington Square today, married and happy, having obtained divorces in South America. With them are the old mother-in-law that Felise would not desert, and little Doris, not so little any more. The husband of Felise and the wife of Maskell, who had stood between them and happiness, live on, without the power to molest them.

But all this lay in the future that night. When all the others had gone and Thatcher Colt and I remained alone in the library of the Police Commissioner, I congratulated my chief, and he smiled a little sadly.

"Tony," he confessed, "I feel lonesome tonight. Everybody has gone home except you and me—and a little girl waiting downstairs—Betty."

"Really?"

"Will you two join me in a little supper—or would you rather be to yourselves?"

We ate our supper, Betty and I, as the guests of Thatcher Colt in his little house on Seventieth Street, and Betty would let me have only two glasses of that priceless port. She said that from then on she intended to manage me. And I've always found her a girl of her word.

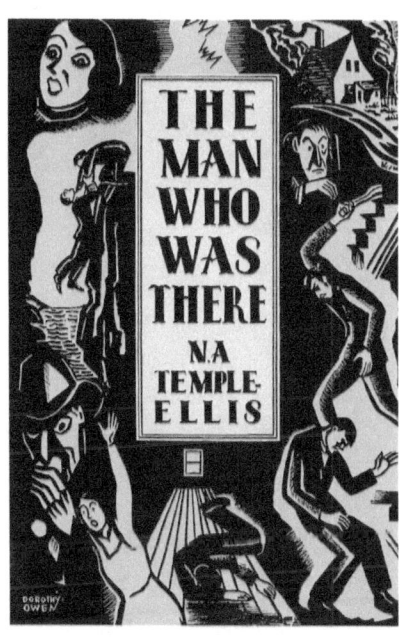

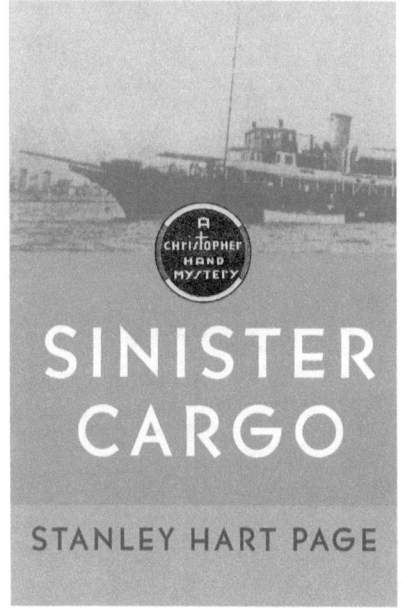

COACHWHIP PUBLICATIONS

COACHWHIPBOOKS.COM

FEAR OF FEAR

FLORENCE RYERSON
COLIN CLEMENTS

THE DESERT LAKE MYSTERY

KAY CLEAVER STRAHAN
Author of THE DESERT MOON MYSTERY

THE STUDIO
MURDER MYSTERY
THE EDINGTONS

MURDER
THROUGH THE WINDOW

FRANCIS EVERTON

COACHWHIP PUBLICATIONS
COACHWHIPBOOKS.COM

COACHWHIP PUBLICATIONS

COACHWHIPBOOKS.COM

CLUES OF THE CARIBBEES
being certain criminal investigations
of Henry Poggioli
T. S. Stribling

MURDER
IN A WALLED TOWN
KATHERINE WOODS

VULTURES
IN THE SKY
A HUGH RENNERT MYSTERY

TODD DOWNING

LOUIS F. BOOTH
THE BANK VAULT MYSTERY
BROKERS' END

COACHWHIP PUBLICATIONS
COACHWHIPBOOKS.COM

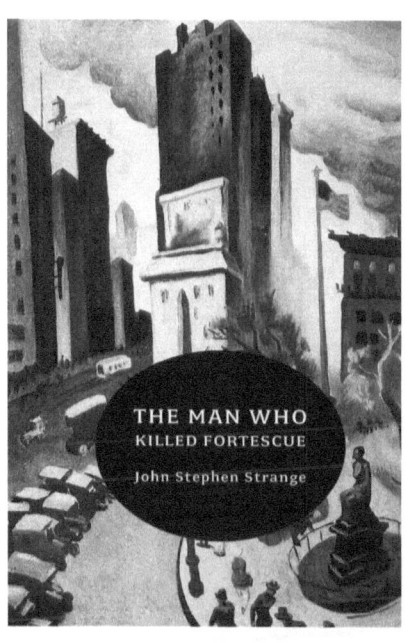

THE MAN WHO
KILLED FORTESCUE
John Stephen Strange

HENRY JAMES FORMAN
THE REMBRANDT
MURDER

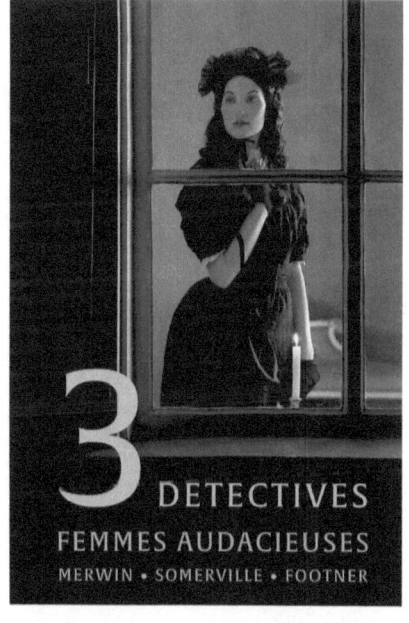

3 DETECTIVES
FEMMES AUDACIEUSES
MERWIN • SOMERVILLE • FOOTNER

MEDORA
FIELD

WHO KILLED
AUNT MAGGIE?

COACHWHIP PUBLICATIONS

COACHWHIPBOOKS.COM

THE MAY DAY MYSTERY

OCTAVUS ROY COHEN

The Jekyll-Hyde Murder Case

MADELON ST. DENIS

VIRGINIA RATH

DEATH AT DAYTON'S FOLLY

THE 5.18 MYSTERY

J Jefferson Farjeon

COACHWHIP PUBLICATIONS

COACHWHIPBOOKS.COM

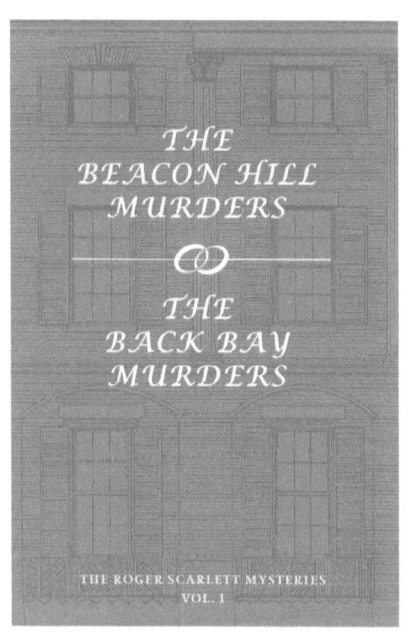

THE
BEACON HILL
MURDERS

THE
BACK BAY
MURDERS

THE ROGER SCARLETT MYSTERIES
VOL. 1

THE
SARA ELIZABETH
MASON
MYSTERIES

MURDER RENTS A ROOM

THE CRIMSON FEATHER

HELEN BURNHAM

THE MURDER OF
LALLA LEE

THE TELLTALE
TELEGRAM

THOMAS KINDON

MURDER
IN THE
MOOR

COACHWHIP PUBLICATIONS

COACHWHIPBOOKS.COM